FIRE STORM

Read more about Michael and Katya's adventures in:

SOS ADVENTURE

FIRE STORM

COLIN BATEMAN

Hodder
Children's
Books

A division of Hachette Children's Books

For Matthew

Copyright © 2010 Colin Bateman
First published in Great Britain in 2010
by Hodder Children's Books

The right of Colin Bateman to be identified as the Author of
the Work has been asserted by him in accordance with the
Copyright, Designs and Patents Act 1988

2

A Catalogue record for this book is available from the British Library

ISBN-13: 978 0 340 99887 8

Typeset in AGaramond by Avon DataSet Ltd,
Bidford on Avon, Warwickshire

Printed and bound in Great Britain by
CPI Bookmarque Ltd, Croydon, Surrey

The paper and board used in this paperback by Hodder Children's Books
are natural recyclable products made from wood grown in
sustainable forests. The manufacturing processes conform to the
environmental regulations of the country of origin.

Hodder Children's Books
a division of Hachette Children's Books
338 Euston Road, London NW1 3BH
An Hachette UK company
www.hachette.co.uk

Prologue: The Chase

New Ireland, Bismarck Archipelago, Papua New Guinea
3°20'S 152°00'E

Joe Kabui was running for his life.

He could hardly breathe. He had been running for hours, stopping only occasionally, hoping against hope that he had lost his pursuers in the dense undergrowth. But they were good. Very good. And determined.

Joe was the chief of the village. He was fourteen years old. He had been chief for less than twenty-four hours. His father, chief before him, had been murdered. Because Joe was just a boy his killers had expected him to cave in to their demands. But he had said no to them, and in so doing he had doomed himself and his village.

They had emerged from the dawn mist. Even though they wore the masks of the Duk-Duk secret society, the very people who were supposed to keep law and order on their island, Joe knew they were imposters. His father had been chief of the Tolai people, a wise man and a high priest of the Duk-Duk, and Joe had been brought up in their traditions, which went back for thousands of years. Duk-Duk might wear hideous cane and fibre masks, and capes of woven leaves which would spread out behind them like giant bats, but they certainly didn't wear bandoliers of ammunition strapped across their chests or carry Kalashnikov rifles. They did not set fire to houses and destroy fishing boats. They did not kill anyone who stood up to them. They were supposed to be a force for good.

Joe had no idea if his mother was still alive. All he knew was that the bandits were not going to give up. Once he was dead there would be nobody else left to stand up to them, and the land would be theirs. All along the coast other villages had given in to the bandits and sold their tribal lands for a paltry sum, but Joe's father had inspired his people to say no, and now he and they were paying for it with their lives.

At first Joe kept to the treeline along the beaches, but he was spotted, and a bullet cracked into an overhanging rock centimetres from his head. Then, slowly working his way inland, he found himself on the outskirts of another village, but word had clearly spread, because they were waiting for him there, their ambush set. It only failed because a crocodile had suddenly emerged from the undergrowth, intent merely on slipping back into one of the dozens of rivers which formed the road networks of the rainforest, but it was enough of a shock to cause the hidden gunman to shoot at it in panic.

Joe had no choice but to go deeper still into the rainforest. He had grown up in and around it, and knew as much about living off it as anyone else on the island, but he also knew that you could never truly *know* the rainforest, or second-guess it, because it always threw the unexpected at you.

It was so dark and dense that it was impossible to see very far in any direction, and it was possible to imagine that he had given the bandits the slip, but he knew better. They had trackers with them. They could read the signs. A broken twig here. A vague toe-print there. Joe waded across streams and along them until the leeches drove him out. He had to waste precious time picking the engorged bloodsuckers off his arms, legs and back, and delve down into his pants looking for them. As he reached up to a branch to help support him as he crossed another stream, it suddenly came to life in his hands, a black snake at least two metres in length. Its fangs snapped out at him and it was only his well-honed reflexes that allowed him to avert an agonizing death as his own hand shot out and slapped it away.

The bandits kept up their dogged pursuit throughout the day. As Joe moved inland the ground began to rise. The island was long and narrow, in some places only ten kilometres wide, with a rugged, steep and mountainous spine dominated by the dark and brooding Mount Taron.

His legs ached. His yellow T-shirt hung raggedly from him. The soles of his bare feet were as tough as any pair of shoes, but the relentless chase was taking its toll. They were cut and bleeding and sore. Fungus spores filled the air. Mosquitoes hummed around him. He had no clear idea of where he was going, or where he might find sanctuary – all he knew was that his father had sworn to him that the mountain was home to spirits that would protect true members of the Duk-Duk. Joe wasn't sure if he believed in any of the old stories, but he had nothing else left. There was a stench now as well, which had been growing for hours.

It was like rotten eggs – but millions and millions of them. It seeped into his pores and made him want to retch. He felt dizzy and disorientated. Was he still going up the mountain, or sideways, or even down? It felt like the ground was moving under him.

He paused to drink from a stream. When he gulped at the water he was surprised to find it so warm. Before he could even begin to think about *that*, there was an ominous click. His eyes flitted up.

Barely a dozen metres in front of him.

Bandits. Their guns raised.

They had outflanked him as the rising gradient punished his legs and slowed him down. Or they might have been from a different group, one that had come right over the mountain.

It didn't matter. He was dead for sure.

There was no sign of the Duk-Duk masks now, but their faces remained hidden, cloaked in chalk powder and streaked with sweat. Their hair was as wild as Joe's, but their eyes were wide, bloodshot and drug-fuelled. He knew what they were – mercenaries, being paid to remove a troublesome tribal chief and grab his land. They were loyal to no one. He wouldn't be captured, there would be no charges, no trial, not even any final request or last words. They would execute him and leave him to be consumed by the forest. In a matter of hours he would just be a collection of bones.

Joe slowly regained his feet. He wasn't going to accept death like a trapped animal. He would stand, proud and defiant to the end. Yet as he stood he felt suddenly shaky again, and almost toppled over.

But then he saw that it wasn't only him. The bandits themselves had involuntarily lowered their guns and were struggling to stay on their feet.

The ground itself was moving.

There was a loud ripping sound and huge cracks suddenly appeared in the mountainside. One of the bandits yelled and took a step back as one appeared before him, but immediately fell into another behind.

And then from above, from the very summit of the mountain, rocks began to hail down; huge molten boulders exploding in the vegetation like mortar shells. The bandits turned and fled. One took a direct hit. His screams were horrific as he lay crushed and burning.

A flaming boulder landed beside Joe, showering him with shards of molten rock. He patted frantically at his hair and clothes, trying to extinguish the flames.

There was a massive boom from above. Joe looked

up at the mountain, but where before he had had a clear view of the summit, now it was masked in smoke. More rocks began to rain down, all around him.

Joe sprang forward with every ounce of strength that remained in his exhausted muscles. He had been chased by bandits all day – but now it felt as if he was being chased by an entire mountain.

Chapter One

They hardly had time to catch their breath. One minute they were lost in the icy wastes of the Arctic, the next they were swooping over an island of dank, impenetrable rainforests and craggy unexplored mountain ranges. New Ireland was one of the largest islands in the Bismarck Archipelago, off the north-eastern coast of Papua New Guinea.

Obviously, Michael Monroe had never heard of it.

He was fourteen years of age, an orphan and a former troublemaker who had been expelled from more schools than he could remember. Lately he had become the newest member of the globe-trotting environmental rescue service, SOS, and had been hailed as a hero for helping to recover a lost satellite.

Obviously, given that he was a hero, Michael Monroe was never going to admit one basic fact to his colleagues: he didn't much like spiders.

But his young comrade Katya knew already. They had barely been off the helicopter for five minutes, and were helping to move supplies into their new headquarters at the small airport on the outskirts of the island's only large town, Kavieng, when the spider, no bigger than Michael's thumbnail, leapt from a computer monitor on to his hand and he let out a shriek that others might have reserved for an encounter with a large sea monster or a carnivorous alien. It hadn't attacked him, and it didn't bite him. It was just using him as a means of getting from one place to another. But his yell suggested that it had plunged its fangs into his vein and transferred a poison that would paralyse in a matter of seconds. Michael swiped it off his hand with a shudder and then glanced around at Katya.

'I . . .' he began.

'You big scaredy cat!' Katya exclaimed.

'I'm not . . . I didn't . . . it just . . .'

'You're scared of spiders!'

'It was just the shock of it . . .' Michael mumbled.

'Michael Monroe, do you know how many different types of insects there are in the rainforest on this island?'

'Uhm . . . a few dozen?' he asked hopefully.

'One million,' said Katya. 'And those are just the ones they've discovered.' She stood in front of him and said, 'So if I were you, I would start getting used to them. Here, I saved you one of my sweets.'

She held out her hand.

He held out his.

She dropped the same spider right back into it.

Michael screamed again, hurled the spider into the air, and swore loud and bloody vengeance as she danced out of the tent, laughing hysterically.

Dr Jimmy Kincaid, the pop star turned founder of SOS, called the Artists to a meeting just as the sun dipped out of the sky. Michael wasn't sure if he was invited or not. He had, after all, only recently signed up with SOS, and was still very much finding his feet. The Action Response Team was a small, elite unit within the organization, a group of specialists trained to solve any problem and dive headfirst into any crisis; Michael, on the other hand, specialized in nothing, and most of the crisis he had dived headfirst into had been of his own making. His exploits in the Arctic had undoubtedly worked in his favour, but nobody had actually said anything to him about becoming an

Artist. Even Katya, who was an expert in several fields, wasn't certain of her own place in the team.

From the outside, the compound where SOS was setting up was little more than a collection of army surplus tents, a hastily constructed helicopter pad, several generators, dozens of boxes of supplies and a high wire fence to keep out inquisitive locals. But if they had been able to peek through the tent flaps they would have seen a hi-tech base to rival anything the world's elite military forces could come up with. 3D television screens seemed to hang in the air, satellite feeds gave stunning views of the entire Bismarck Archipelago, weather maps showed systems moving back and forth across the Indian and Pacific Oceans, local, national and international television news kept the team up to date on other world trouble spots, there were live video conferences going on from SOS bases on every continent . . . Michael still wasn't used to how efficient the whole operation was. They'd only been on the ground for a couple of hours and the SOS machine was already running smoothly; in that time Michael had carried a few boxes of supplies and struggled to find a charger for his iPod.

Now he hovered just outside the Artists' tent; it was set out with fold-down chairs, and a small bank of monitors. The flap was open, but with a mosquito net hanging across it. He could see a criss-cross version of Dr Kincaid already talking. Mr Crown, the burly, shaven-headed all-action member of the team, was seated directly in front of him; to his left was Bailey, the helicopter pilot who was either the bravest in the business or the most reckless, depending on your point of view. Certainly he had 'lost' a number of aircraft. Next to Bailey was Bonsoir, their linguistics expert and chief strategic planner. On the other side of Mr Crown sat Dr Faustus, their surgeon, a man who had reputedly carried out a heart transplant while fighting off a bear. Katya was sitting just behind them. She glanced back at him once, and smirked.

'Michael, are you not joining us?' It was Dr Kincaid. Everyone turned.

Michael pulled the mosquito net back and stood awkwardly in the entrance. 'Ahm . . .'

There were no empty chairs.

'Katya?'

Her head snapped to Dr Kincaid. 'Yip?'

'Did I not ask you to put out chairs for the Artists?'

'Yes. I did.'

'You seem to have miscounted.'

'No, I . . .' And then she understood what Dr

Kincaid was saying. 'I didn't think he . . .'

'Good try,' said Dr Kincaid. 'Now why don't you nip out and get him one?'

'But . . .'

'Michael, in the meantime, you can take Katya's.'

Katya got up and strode furiously past him. She didn't make eye contact, but he was quite sure she could see the smile on his face.

Michael took her seat. He nodded around the other Artists. Did it mean he was one of them? They were nodding back, but they were smirking as well, the way you would if a child put on a fancy-dress police uniform. It didn't mean he actually was one. They were indulging him. Or were they? He knew there was a simple solution: just ask.

Am I an Artist?

The problem with that, of course, was that they would most probably say no, you're just here to get the coffee.

So he kept silent and fixed his eyes on the screen hanging just above Dr Kincaid. There was a still photograph on it of a woman with short grey hair, a small, sharp nose, bright blue eyes and a friendly smile. She had a monkey in her arms.

'Michael, for your benefit, this is Dr Anna Roper.

The one with the smile, that is.' Katya reappeared and plumped her chair down as far away from Michael as possible. 'Dr Roper is the reason for our visit to New Ireland.'

'This is the missing scientist?' Michael asked.

Katya rolled her eyes.

Dr Kincaid said, 'Yes, Dr Roper is missing, lost, gone mad, drowned, or, on the other hand, she may be perfectly fine. The fact is that her expedition set out two weeks ago, and everything was fine for the first six days, and then suddenly radio contact was lost, and nobody has heard a word from her since. We're here to find her.'

'Nearly nine thousand square kilometres of dense rainforest to search,' said Bonsoir. 'Shouldn't be hard.'

'Chopper's of damn-all use,' said Bailey. 'Canopy's so thick, you can't see a thing from the air.'

'There's every parasite known to man, and plenty that aren't, out there,' said Dr Faustus, 'and she didn't take much more than a first aid kit with her. If she's been bitten by something, or caught some disease, I don't hold out much hope.'

'It's not her getting lost or the bugs or the snakes that worries me,' said Mr Crown. 'It's the cannibals.'

'Cannibals?' said Michael.

'Now . . . now,' said Dr Kincaid, 'we don't know that there are—'

'We have good evidence there are tribes out there that still haven't had any contact with civilization. Previous experience suggests that such tribes continue to practise cannibal—'

'The point,' Dr Kincaid cut in firmly, 'is that the sooner we find Dr Roper the better. Agreed?' The Artists nodded. 'Good. Now let's work out the details of how we're going to . . .' He stopped. He had noticed Michael slowly raising his hand. 'Yes, Michael?'

'Ahm – excuse me . . . but . . . we've just been to the Arctic, and now we've flown halfway around the world to undertake something that sounds every bit as dangerous. I just wanted to know . . . you know . . . what's so important about Dr Roper that she needs SOS to save her?'

Michael was aware of Katya rolling her eyes again.

Dr Kincaid nodded. 'Michael, a very good question, and of course you missed the beginning of our meeting. Dr Roper is carrying out vital research. The rainforest here on the island is owned by different tribes, different villages, but they're poor people with no access to proper medical facilities. So they're selling the land to loggers, or in some cases they're being forced to sell it, and the loggers are cutting down the rainforest. If it continues at the current rate, within five years there'll be nothing left. And that pattern, my friend, is being repeated all over the planet. If the rainforest goes, not only will a quarter of all species become extinct, and I'm talking about everything from butterflies to beetles to spiders to snakes to lizards to frogs to toads to parrots to sloths, but things are going to get a hell of a lot warmer as well. About thirty per cent of the greenhouse gases released into the atmosphere are caused by deforestation.'

'But her research is . . . ?'

'Parts of this island have never been explored. If she can discover some previously unknown species of animal, hopefully something furry and cute, then the publicity that gets will hopefully convince the government to declare the whole island a national park, and that'll stop the loggers dead in their tracks. That's why she's gone out there, in my humble opinion – barely equipped, badly supplied, inexpertly guided and at the mercy of disease, cannibals, unknown creatures and developers. But I do know one thing. If there's a creature like that to be found, she's pig-headed enough to keep going until she finds it, and if she finds it we might just turn the tide against these damn loggers. So now do you understand?'

'Yes, sir,' said Michael.

'And did I mention that Dr Roper is my sister?'

Chapter Two

It was too muggy for sleep. And too *loud*. Michael was exhausted, but every time he closed his eyes the buzz of insects woke him up. The nets were fine for keeping the mosquitoes out, but that didn't account for the creatures that were already in the tent, or who found their way in through different means. He was bitten, and he was bitten, and he was bitten. They all were.

'I hate this place,' he said, swinging gently on his hammock.

Katya was next to him. She said, 'You ain't seen nothing yet. It's a jungle out there. Well, a rainforest.'

They had been given their own small tent. The Artists were still up, planning, while they had been ordered to bed.

'We're not children,' Katya had fumed.

'Technically . . .' Bonsoir had commented.

'You can't make us.'

'You think not?' Mr Crown had said.

He had picked her up, carried her across the compound, and placed her headfirst into a barrel of fresh fish. Her yells and screams caused much laughter. While she was still struggling to get out, Mr Crown turned to Michael and said, 'What about you?'

Michael faked a yawn and said he was more than ready to retire.

'You still smell of fish,' Michael said. She had hosed herself down about twelve times in an effort to get rid of the stink. 'Or maybe it's your perfume.'

'At least I stood up to them.'

'And lost. You should choose your battles more carefully.'

In the darkness, a shoe hit him on the forehead.

An hour later, they were both still twisting and turning. Michael said, 'Did you know Dr Kincaid had a sister?'

'Nope.'

'Do you think it's right, doing this?'

'Doing what?'

'Using SOS for personal reasons.'

'What do you mean?'

'I mean, there are emergencies all over the planet, but here we all are, looking for one person.'

'She's important. Didn't you listen?'

'I listened. I'm just thinking out loud.'

'Well, don't.'

They were quiet for a little while. Then Michael said, 'You know what's going to happen, don't you?'

'I'm trying to sleep.'

'We're only going to get so far into this, and then once it gets dangerous, they're going to leave us behind.'

'No they won't. Not this time. Not after the Arctic, and the satellite.'

'I know we did well there, but they might not look at it like that. They'll say, oh they only just survived that, let's not put them in the firing line this time. They're going to have us doing something really boring. Paperwork, probably.'

'If they try to make me do paperwork . . .'

'I suppose I can get used to the smell of fish.'

'He took me by surprise. It won't happen again.'

Michael remained silent.

'It *won't*,' said Katya.

* * *

Because the rainforest canopy blanketed virtually the entire island, it was impossible for the Artists to search from the air the area where Dr Roper was thought to have disappeared. The plan therefore was for Bailey to take them by helicopter along the coast, closely following the Boluminski Highway, as far as Put Put Mission Station. From there they would board three inflatable dinghies and speed up the Sepik River to set up a second base camp in the grounds of St Mark's Mission Station, a church-school-hospital run by an Irish priest, which was, according to Bonsoir, the last outpost of civilization.

'Depending, of course, on what your definition of civilization is,' he added as they boarded the chopper. 'Is it having access to an Xbox 360? Or is it knowing you can drink the water without it killing you?'

'It's a bit early in the morning for philosophical questions,' said Mr Crown.

Bonsoir said, 'It's never too early for philosophical questions.'

Michael grinned as he strapped himself in. There was something exhilarating about being in the company of the Artists. They – the proper Artists that is – joked and wound each other up and had disagreements about virtually everything, but behind it all there was a real camaraderie. Michael knew that every one of them would sacrifice themselves to save a fellow team member, and he hoped that he would do the same.

Although perhaps not for Katya.

He gave her the thumbs-up.

She gave him a scowl.

Dr Faustus said, 'You two be careful. You've had your shots, but they won't protect you from everything. You'll need to drink a lot to keep hydrated, but the water here will kill you unless it's treated. Some of those parasites get into your system and they'll make you miserable for life. There are bacteria and viruses we haven't even heard of and there's no cure for them. So if in doubt, purify. There's tablets in your kit. Don't wander off, don't get lost.'

Michael said, 'Do we look like idiots?'

Dr Faustus looked from one to the other. 'Yes,' he said.

After the barrenness of the Arctic wilderness, the rainforest from the air was incredibly rich and diverse. And the clue to its diversity was very much in its name – *rain*forest. The range of mountains that formed the spine of New Ireland was large enough to have its own weather system, which, when you got all the scientific and technical language out of the way, meant *lots and lots* of rain. Water meant life, and the heat meant that all manner of things multiplied with abandon. In fact the only creature that wasn't really set up for living in the rainforest was supposedly the smartest of them all – man. They were there all right, but life was a struggle. Most of the island's inhabitants lived in communities that hugged the shoreline where the fishing was at least bountiful; those that lived inland struggled from one crisis to the next, existing on a knife edge between starvation, disease and danger. There was, according to Dr Faustus, nothing idyllic about living in a rainforest.

'If you survive down there,' he said, indicating with his thumb out of the open door of the helicopter, 'you're either as tough as nails, or you've eaten someone who's as tough as nails.'

He winked and turned to check his equipment. Katya leant closer to Michael and shouted above the cacophony of the rotor blades: 'He's just trying to scare us. I don't think the island is big enough to have undiscovered cannibal tribes.'

'You're the expert,' said Michael.

She was, he supposed, at least a *bit* of an expert.

Certainly she seemed to spend half her life glued to her computer.

Thinking *that* made Michael worry some more. He could see why they would want to train Katya as an Artist – but not himself. He was expert at nothing. He wasn't particularly interested in researching where he was going to. He didn't speak any languages like Bonsoir and he couldn't fly like Bailey. He could probably handle himself in a fight, but if someone the size of Mr Crown came at him, he would run away. Clearly he knew nothing about medicine. The only Artist he had anything in common with was Dr Kincaid himself – he had no special skills, unless you counted making loads and loads of money, setting up an incredibly successful charity and saving countless lives as a result. Michael's only contribution so far to *this* SOS adventure had been making the coffee.

Bailey's voice was just audible over the clatter of the blades: 'Approaching Put Put Mission Station, landing in two.'

Peering down, Michael caught glimpses through the swirling dust of a white building with a red cross clearly marked on its sloping roof.

And in the yard beside it there were jeeps, trucks and long flat-bed vehicles, with a crowd of men squinting up, one hand protecting their eyes, the other holding their rifles.

'Break out the bulletproof vests,' Bailey announced. 'Looks like we have a welcoming committee!'

Chapter Three

When the blinding clouds of dust finally dissipated the Artists had already disembarked and were unloading their equipment as if nothing was amiss. Only Dr Kincaid paid any attention to the gunmen in front of the Put Put Mission Station. Faces of patients getting treatment inside the mission were pressed to the windows, watching; relatives sat outside, cooking on small stoves; a team of labourers was building a wall a dozen metres away; traffic from the highway kicked up yet more dust. Dr Kincaid had a mobile phone clamped to his ear and was talking into it as he looked the gunmen over. They had a swagger about them and easy familiarity with their guns which suggested they might be ex-military. He casually approached the men, still chatting on his phone, and when one of them started to say something he held up his hand to stop them until he could finish his conversation. Michael had been watching him since they landed, and knew Dr Kincaid hadn't received a call. He was just pretending, just showing them that he didn't think they were that important.

Then he snapped his phone shut and smiled. 'Gentlemen,' he said, 'thank you for coming to welcome us. Are you attached to the mission station?'

Only one of the men wasn't carrying a gun. He was wearing a suit, trainers and a baseball cap. The suit had once been white, but was now flecked with mud. The hems of the trousers were ragged. The others looked to this man to respond. He took his time in the same way that Dr Kincaid had, pausing to light a cigarette, draw in the smoke and puff it out.

'We're not here to welcome you,' he said. His English was perfect. He had the dark skin of a local, but short, dyed blond hair. A gold chain hung around his neck and he had several rings on each hand. 'We're here to advise you to go home.'

'Well, thank you for the advice. We'll certainly take it on board.'

Dr Kincaid turned back to the Artists and began to direct them where to put the supplies they were taking off the chopper. Behind him, the gunmen moved closer.

The man in the whitish suit said, 'We know who you are. We know what you're doing. You think you're helping, but you're not. These people need medicine, and they need education, and they need electricity and clean water. The only way they can get that is selling their land. We're saving them, not you. All you're doing is making life harder for them.'

Dr Kincaid nodded. 'Well, like I say, I'll take your thoughts on board. Now if you don't mind?'

He lifted a box himself and moved it off the chopper. But when he tried to place it with the others, he found his path blocked by the man in the suit.

'We're telling you to get off our island. *Now.*'

Behind him the rest of his men lined up with their guns raised and pointed.

Dr Kincaid took a deep breath. He set the box down. He placed one foot on top and leant on it.

'Well,' he said nonchalantly, 'we're not going anywhere. You want us off, you better start shooting.'

Michael could hardly believe what he was hearing. He became aware of Katya beside him, and wasn't sure if the heart he could hear beating so loudly was hers or his own. Michael would at least have expected the other Artists to stop their unloading and offer moral and physical support to their leader, but they continued

29

their work, and didn't even look towards him.

Dr Kincaid had a quizzical kind of look on his face, as if it was some kind of a joke. Mr Whitesuit stared at him. Beside him the armed men bristled, pumped up, ready for action, but also confused by the lack of reaction from the SOS unit.

To Michael the stand-off felt like it lasted for hours, but it must only have been a matter of seconds until Mr Whitesuit raised his hand, and the men around him reluctantly lowered their rifles.

'You have been warned,' he said.

'Noted,' said Dr Kincaid.

Mr Whitesuit walked away. After a little hesitation his men followed. They climbed back into their vehicles and roared away. It was only then that a priest and three nuns emerged from the mission station and hurried across to the new arrivals. They were full of apologies. They had been ordered to stay inside by the gunmen. They offered coffee.

Dr Kincaid looked across at Michael. 'Usually he gets the coffee,' he said. 'But I guess we can make an exception.'

The nuns turned back to the mission, while the priest volunteered to help with the unloading.

Dr Kincaid studied his mobile phone again.

As he began to tap out a text message, Michael hesitantly approached.

'Dr . . . Dr Kincaid?'

'Mmmmm?'

'What just happened? They were ready to kill us all and you just . . . ignored them.'

Dr Kincaid continued working on his text message for several moments. Then, finished, he smiled at Michael. 'I didn't ignore them, I just didn't rise to the provocation.'

'But what if they started shooting? We would all have been—'

'Michael, son, they had no intention of killing us. They were sent here to warn us off. And it may well be that they try to kill us sometime in the next few days, but they were never going to do it here. For one thing, too many witnesses.' He nodded at the patients, still watching through the mission windows. 'And for another, I'm far too famous. If they killed me here, every news crew in the world would descend on this place, and they'd pretty soon work out who was responsible, and more to the point, who sent them.'

'Who did send them?'

Dr Kincaid smiled. 'It was Frank.'

Michael smiled too. On their way back from the

Arctic they had come up with the name 'Frank' to describe whatever shadowy man or woman, terrorist group, big business concern or unbalanced nation might be responsible for the act of evil they were facing. It was a way of saying that sometimes you just didn't know who was behind everything.

'That Frank, he gets around,' said Michael. 'And this time he's working through the logging companies?'

'That's about it.'

Dr Kincaid turned back towards the helicopter. But Michael wasn't finished. Something the man in the suit had said had stuck in his head, and he couldn't dislodge it.

'Dr Kincaid?'

The doctor stopped just as he was about to climb on board. 'What?'

'It's just . . . I mean . . . what if they have a point? What they were saying about the people here needing water and medicine and . . . stuff. If they need the money, then why not sell their land . . . ?'

Dr Kincaid nodded. 'To tell you the truth, Michael, it's a bit of a grey area. If you're really thirsty, what would you prefer – a few sips of water now, and you're going to be thirsty again in ten minutes, or a well of your own, say, at some unknown point in the future, but you'll have all the water you'll ever need?'

'I . . . I'd like to think I could wait . . . but . . .'

'Exactly. Thirst is thirst. You can't blame these people for selling their land, because they get the money right away. But they don't get much, and once it's gone, it's gone, and so is the rainforest, and not only are they poor again, the whole planet is poor, thirsty and starving. It's tough. But if there's one thing we know about Frank, he's not in it for the good of these people. He may say he's providing a service, but all he's interested in is making money, and once he's taken the trees and reduced this place to a lifeless desert, he'll walk away and look for the next place to destroy. That's why we're here, to help stop that, and part of that is finding my sister. So if you don't mind . . . ?'

Dr Kincaid heaved himself up into the chopper. Michael took hold of another box of supplies and walked them back to where the other Artists were stockpiling them.

He was busy thinking through what Dr Kincaid had said. He was still quite confused by it all. He guessed that there were always grey areas, and that few things were ever simply right or wrong.

Katya placed a box on the pile beside his. He said, 'I

don't think we've seen the last of that lot.'

'I know. The guy in the suit, he just looked . . .'

'Evil,' said Michael.

Katya nodded. 'Evil,' she repeated.

'I don't think I could just have stood there the way Dr Kincaid did. Brave or what?'

'Yeah, I suppose.'

'What do you mean, you *suppose*?'

She smiled. 'No. You're right. He was brave. But it's a little easier to be brave when you have *that* behind you.'

She nodded towards the helicopter. Michael could see Bailey still behind the controls, though the rotation of the blades had long since stopped. He didn't know what she was getting at.

'What do you mean? The heli—?'

'*Look*, for goodness sake. *There*, and *there*, and *there* . . .' He still didn't understand. 'It's a Chinook, an ex-army helicopter. It still has its weapons.' She pointed again. 'Machine guns on either side, rocket launchers, it even has anti-tank missiles. If those gunmen had tried *anything*, Bailey would have blown them all to pieces. And they knew it. So to answer your question, yes, Dr Kincaid was certainly brave. But he had back-up. You *idiot*.'

She walked away, shaking her head. Michael stared at the chopper. Yes, he had to agree.

He was an idiot.

Chapter Four

Michael was feeling a bit useless. The Artists, including Katya, were obviously well drilled and very efficient. They produced compressed air cylinders and rapidly inflated three rubber raiding craft donated by the Royal Navy and fitted outboard diesel motors. Paddles were broken out, to allow a quieter approach to an intended target. Two M16 assault rifles were also issued for each craft, and every Artist wore a Browning Hi-Power 9mm handgun. Even Michael and Katya.

Michael was surprised. 'I've never . . .'

'Katya will teach you,' said Mr Crown, who was in charge of weapons. 'You'll have plenty of time when we get to St Mark's.'

Michael knew what *that* meant. While the Artists set off in search of Dr Roper, he and Katya *once again* would be left behind at the mission station with orders to interact with the local community. While the Artists were having all kinds of adventures searching for Dr Kincaid's missing sister, *their* mission would be to learn about life in the rainforest, to help in the school or hospital, and to pass on the SOS ecological and environmental ethos.

It wasn't fair.

No, it *was* fair. He knew that, deep down. He wasn't expert at *anything*, apart from pig-headedness and cheek. If he wanted to become a proper and full member of the elite SOS squad he would need to show patience, learn the ropes and do what he was told, no matter how frustrating it was. And he had to remember that just a few days previously he had been holed up in a freezing cold boarding school, bored out of his head. SOS had rescued him from that, taken him on an amazing adventure in the Arctic, and now here he was, about to zip upriver in a tropical rainforest teeming with wild and dangerous creatures (and quite possibly gunmen), and with a handgun strapped to his waist and an assault rifle within easy reach. What did he have to complain about?

Besides, he had an instinctive feeling that even if they were left behind at St Mark's Mission Station, *something* would happen. Even Bailey was aware of it.

As they loaded the rubber boats he said, 'Face it, Michael, you're what we call a crap-magnet. You don't have to go looking for trouble, trouble will find you.'

'Is that a good thing?'

'No,' said Bailey.

Dr Kincaid decided who would go in which boat. He and Bonsoir would lead the way. Mr Crown, Dr Faustus and Bailey would man the second. Michael and Katya would take the third.

That, at least, was good news. They were being trusted with their own craft.

Mr Crown did not look very impressed. 'No messing about. If those supplies go in the water, you're going in after them. And try not to shoot yourself.'

'I'll keep an eye on him,' said Katya.

'I'm talking about you as well,' snapped Mr Crown.

It was just after noon when they set off along the Sepik River, heading for St Mark's to set up their forward HQ. Dr Kincaid's inflatable raced ahead, with Bailey piloting the second close behind and Katya in control of the third doing her best to keep up. It was hot. It was sticky. The river water was sluggish, thick and brown and as they sped along it was joined by hundreds of streams and waterfalls flowing down off the island's mountainous spine.

Michael and Katya didn't talk much. Most of their conversation went like this:

'Can I have a go now?'

'No.'

'Can I have a go now?'

'No.'

'Can I have a go now?'

'Not yet.'

'Give me a go now.'

'No.'

'Give me a go or I'll throw you in the river.'

'Yeah, good luck with that.'

'I swear to—'

'I'll give you a go in ten minutes.'

Ten minutes passed.

'Ten minutes is up.'

'Not by my watch.'

'Ten minutes is definitely up. Give me a go.'

'No.'

'You still smell of fish.'

'You're *definitely* not getting a go.'

She did, eventually, let him take over. He'd barely been at the controls for two minutes when she said, 'It's my turn now.'

Now that he was actually in control he could see why she was so keen to get back to it. It was *fun*. They weren't cruising, they were racing. The river was wide at first, then noticeably thinner, with the tree canopy in many places joining together above them, blocking out the sun.

Insects kept dropping down on them.

An hour into their journey and with Michael enjoying his second stint at the controls, the sound of their engines disturbed a colony of sleeping fruit bats and they exploded out of the branches, thousands of them swooping in and around them. One got caught in Katya's hair and she let out a scream and began beating at it. Michael, ducking down to avoid getting smacked in the face, cut their speed right down and let go of the controls so that he could move forward to help disentangle the bat.

'Get it off me!' Katya was wearing a baseball cap, but with her ponytail protruding from the back, and it was in this that the squeaking flapping little creature had entangled itself.

Michael tried to get hold of it, but it was putting up a violent struggle.

'Keep still!'

'I am!'

'I'm talking to the bat!'

'Aooow, hurry!'

'I'm doing my best!'

He finally got a proper hold of it, clutching its minuscule torso firmly in one hand and peeling back its claws from the strands of Katya's hair as gently as he could with the other.

But obviously not gently enough.

'Aow! Agh! You're doing that on purp—!'

Then it suddenly came free. Michael threw the bat into the air and it immediately shot up into the branches above.

'Thank you,' Katya hissed, 'even if you did take your time.' She shook her hair out and shuddered. 'Bats, I hate bats.'

Michael laughed. 'With me and spiders, and you and bats, I think we may be in the wrong place.'

She didn't find that funny *at all*, but before she could respond the inflatable gave a sudden lurch. Without the forward thrust they were being drawn into a whirlpool which had formed at the base of one of the larger waterfalls.

Michael stumbled back to the engine and tried to ramp up the power, but instead of leaping forward it gave a sickly cough and died. The inflatable was in the grip of the swirling current, forcing it round and round, while the cascading water from above began drenching them and their supplies. It was already a good ten centimetres deep on the floor of their craft.

'Try it again!' Katya yelled.

'I've tried it! I can't!'

'The paddles! Try the paddles!'

'It's too strong!'

In their panic they had entirely forgotten their comrades.

'Catch this!' Mr Crown yelled; he was at the front of his inflatable, a thin nylon rope in his hand with a small weight on the end. Bailey was steering the boat just far enough away so that it wouldn't be sucked in by the whirlpool, but close enough to allow Mr Crown to throw the rope. Michael caught it, but immediately it slipped through his fingers. Their inflatable sank a little lower. Mr Crown hauled the rope back in as Bailey turned the boat and then aimed it back upstream, taking it past the whirlpool again and steering it into a better position. This time when Mr Crown hurled the rope, it was Katya who caught and quickly secured it. Moments later Bailey gunned his engine and their inflatable was dragged clear of the whirlpool.

Their relief was short-lived. One look at Mr Crown's

face was enough to tell them that their survival was insignificant compared to the damage they might have caused to the inflatable, its engine and the now waterlogged supplies.

They were towed to the river bank, and then along it until they could find a suitable place to stop, all the while baling out the water sloshing around their feet.

When they finally found the right spot, Bailey brought his craft close to shore first. Mr Crown leapt out with his automatic rifle raised and dropped to one knee on the low sand bank. He scanned for any sign of danger, although it was difficult to see very far through the tangle of trees. Satisfied, he slowly rose and waded chest deep back into the river to help land first his own, then Michael and Katya's craft, and finally Dr Kincaid's.

Michael and Katya hurriedly unloaded their supplies before upending the craft to get the remaining water out. Then they turned rather sheepishly, expecting to get a rollicking from Mr Crown for losing control of their inflatable.

But they were the least of his worries.

Mr Crown had ripped off his shirt to reveal a barrelled chest almost completely covered in bloodsucking leeches.

Chapter Five

'You should have known better than to go into the water,' said Dr Faustus.

'Whatever you say, Doc. Just get them off.'

Michael and Katya were watching, fascinated. Mr Crown pointed a finger at them. 'Don't think I've forgotten about you pair,' he warned.

Katya, who had known Mr Crown for a lot longer than Michael, didn't seem especially perturbed. She came right up to him and poked at one of the leeches. Emboldened by this, Michael moved up beside her. The leeches looked *disgusting*.

'They are not disgusting,' said Katya, at which point Michael became aware that he had spoken aloud. 'They're incredible. They bite into you, they fill up and then they just fall off so that they can digest the blood. It's like calling into a garage for petrol.'

'That's what I said,' said Michael. 'Disgusting.'

'If I'd been practising a couple of hundred years ago,' said Dr Faustus, 'they would have been part of my medical kit. Doctors used to be big into draining blood to get rid of infections.'

'But not any more?' Michael asked, as Dr Faustus shook his head. 'Why not?'

'Because they were a bit rubbish. The problem with these little devils is (a) getting them off, and (b) dealing with whatever they infect you with. They all carry parasites, but they're not a danger to humans. The problem lies with whoever they might have been feeding off *before* they got to Mr Crown. They re-transmit whatever was in the last dose of blood, and that might have been months ago. Hepatitis is one, HIV another.' Dr Faustus nodded at Mr Crown. 'You're going to need a whole battery of shots.'

'Then quit explaining the obvious and get on with it.'

'I've seen this in movies,' said Michael. 'The hero has to burn off the leeches with a cigar.'

'Yep,' said Dr Faustus, 'that's one way. One way to kill yourself. It's such a shock to the system that not only does the leech let go, it also vomits the contents of its stomach into the wound it has just caused, and believe you me, you don't want that. Nope, simplest and cleanest way to do it is just to use your fingernail to break the seal of the oral sucker at the thinner end . . . like this . . . and then you repeat it at the posterior . . . and then you just . . . flick . . .'

The leech shot up into the air and landed on the ground, half engorged and twisting around.

'Simple enough, don't you think?' the doctor asked, looking at Michael and Katya.

Michael nodded warily.

'Good, now you can take over.'

'But—'

'Just do it,' snapped Mr Crown.

It took them twenty minutes of prying and flicking. Michael and Katya's fingers and nails were thick with Crown blood and leech ooze, and both of them felt ill. Mr Crown said nothing throughout. Even when they moved behind him, they were convinced that he had eyes in the back of his head, still glaring at them.

Just as they finished, Dr Kincaid let out a shout of excitement. While they had been picking leeches, and Bailey and Bonsoir were checking the flooded engine and the state of the supplies, the SOS founder had broken out a fishing rod and perched himself on the river bank. Michael supposed that this was one of the benefits of being the founder – while others worked, he could relax. But he was trying to land something that was clearly *huge*, and it was putting up quite a fight. Although he was slowly winching it in, he didn't quite have the strength to get it up the last few metres on to the bank.

'She's a beauty!' Dr Kincaid shouted. 'Strong as a . . . ! Someone have a net?'

A fishing net was not something anyone had thought to bring. But it wasn't required.

Thirty seconds after having the last of his leeches removed, Mr Crown strode straight back into the river, took hold of the furiously struggling fish and threw it up on to the river bank.

They all stood looking at it as it flapped about, frantically gasping for air.

'It's a New Guinea Black Bass!' cried Dr Kincaid. 'The toughest freshwater fish on this planet, been after one of these babies for years!'

'Well, now that you have it,' said Katya, 'shouldn't you throw it back into the—'

Before she could finish Mr Crown strode up, his automatic rifle in his hand, and brought the butt of it down hard on the fish's head, killing it instantly.

'Ugh!' Katya exclaimed. 'There was no need to do that!'

'It's a fish,' said Mr Crown, 'and it's lunchtime. Now you have a choice – you can either gut it and start cooking it, or you can get these damn leeches off my legs.'

Katya looked from the fish to Mr Crown and his fresh coating of leeches. Then she threw her arms up in the air and shouted: 'Do it your bloody self!' and stormed away.

There was, of course, nowhere to storm away to. She went about a dozen metres into the rainforest, then backed out of it. It was dark and dank and alive. Instead she stood by the inflatable as Bailey returned to work on it. Dr Faustus began to remove Mr Crown's latest set of leeches while Dr Kincaid set up a small gas cooker and boned the fish. Michael stood over him. He wasn't particularly squeamish, and once it started cooking, and various spices were added to the mix, it smelt fantastic.

'Nothing beats a fish you've caught yourself,' said Dr Kincaid, grinning up at Michael. He glanced across at Katya, standing with her arms folded and still looking furious. 'And don't worry about her. She knows

48

the score. If it was something rare, sure, I'd throw it back, but it's a Black Bass, they're not in short supply. You ever see *The Lion King*?'

'The cartoon?'

'The *animated feature*. You'll know the song then, the one about the circle of life. That's all this is.'

'But we brought food with us, we didn't need to . . .'

'Michael. If God had meant us to be vegetarians he wouldn't have created the Big Mac. Hey, Katya!'

He waved her over. Katya gave him a sullen, defiant look.

He waved her again. She blew air out of her cheeks. She unfolded her arms and tramped across. She looked down at the fish.

'It's the circle of life,' said Michael.

'Shut your face,' said Katya.

'Easy now, *children*. So, tell me, while I fry this delicious specimen, what happened with the inflatable, which nearly cost us not only one of our means of transport, but our supplies and two very junior members of the Action Response Team?'

Katya jabbed a finger at Michael. 'It was him. He lost control of the boat.'

'To help you,' said Michael.

'You *never* lose control.'

'You had a bat in your hair. You were screaming for help.'

'You should have ignored me.'

Michael took a deep breath. He should have pushed her in the water. That would certainly have dislodged the bat, and given her some leeches to keep her happy. But he wasn't going to say that – and for the most unusual reason.

He gave a slight nod of his head. 'She's right.'

She looked at him. 'There's no need for sarcasm.'

'I'm serious. I shouldn't have. I'm sure the bat wasn't very pleasant, but I jeopardized both our lives, and the boat itself, and the supplies. I shouldn't have allowed the power to drop. We were sucked into the whirlpool because of what I did. I'm sorry.'

Katya looked genuinely surprised. 'Well. I'm sorry too. I shouldn't have reacted to the bat like that.'

Dr Kincaid nodded from one to the other. 'Well,' he said, 'looks like we're making some kind of progress here. Almost makes getting pulled into the whirlpool worthwhile.'

Behind them the engine Bailey had been working on suddenly spluttered into life, almost choked a couple of times, and then settled into a good and healthy rhythmic hum.

'It just keeps getting better and better,' Dr Kincaid grinned, 'and the fish is still to come!'

Dr Kincaid was right. The fish was delicious. Katya even had a little bit. And then a little bit more.

'Doesn't make it right,' she said quietly.

Michael said, 'That apology. I didn't mean it.'

'I know. Mine neither.'

'It got us out of trouble.'

'So did mine.'

'You screamed like a girl.'

'I am a girl. And you nearly drowned us.'

'Next time I'll leave you to the bat. *Oooh my hair, ooh my hair.*'

'Grow up,' said Katya.

Bonsoir washed the plates in the river and then packed the cooker away. Michael and Katya returned the supplies to the inflatable. Only a few had actually been ruined. SOS had been making journeys like this for years. Everything they carried had to be transported in waterproof containers.

Soon they pushed the inflatables back in and recommenced their journey upriver. Michael had half expected that their craft would be moved from the back to the middle of their little flotilla, and was relieved when Dr Kincaid (or Mr Crown) raised no objection to them taking up their original position. Despite what he'd said to Katya about the apology, Michael knew he was in the wrong. He wanted to be an Artist. He wanted them to be able to trust him, to know that he wouldn't let them down in a sticky situation.

This time they took it in turns to steer, twenty-minute shifts, no arguing or fighting. In fact, they didn't speak. Best behaviour.

Michael was just taking over for his third go when he saw that Bonsoir, at the front, and then Bailey, had cut their engines. Mr Crown signalled for Michael to cut his. Bonsoir and Dr Kincaid's craft was already halfway around a bend in the river, so could see more of what was coming ahead. Mr Crown broke out the paddles, handing one to Bailey, and they quickly rowed to catch up. Katya did the same, and within a minute all three boats were parallel and stationary just where the bend straightened out to give them their first and proper view of St Mark's Mission Station.

It was burning.

Chapter Six

St Mark's wasn't just a single building, but a whole series of them. One was painted with a red cross. Another was clearly a school, with children steaming out of it, orderly but panicked at the same time. The largest was definitely a church, and it was the one that was burning. Michael caught glimpses of a bell, glinting in the late afternoon sun, through the black smoke which enveloped its small tower. Nurses, doctors, patients, relatives, tradesmen and passing locals had formed a line and were passing water up to the church. A rotund priest was directing where to throw it, but their buckets and plastic containers were too small to be effective; half their contents were spilt before they even reached the fire.

Mr Crown was the first ashore. Typically he didn't wait to beach his craft, but leapt out and waded through the water and up the muddy river bank. He whipped out his Browning handgun. He scanned for danger as he ran, registering the size of the fire, the number of civilians and the casualties stretched out on the ground being attended to by nurses. Before the three craft behind him could land Mr Crown turned to them and made a circling motion with his finger.

'Bring them in about ninety degrees, about three metres out, and shift every kilo you have to the front!'

Michael didn't know what he was doing, but Katya seemed to grasp it immediately. As she turned the craft around Michael moved everything they had quickly and efficiently, then rested his own weight on top. As he did the back of the inflatable raised itself very slightly out of the water. The other two boats lined up beside him also lifted up.

'Now gun those engines!' Mr Crown yelled.

Katya, Bonsoir and Bailey gave their engines full throttle, and immediately three sprays of water shot up into the air and began to rain down on the burning church. Mr Crown observed for a moment, then jumped back into the river and physically moved each of the inflatables into slightly better positions, with two of the resulting funnels of water directly addressing the burning roof and the other pouring down on to the flaming tower.

Within five minutes the fire was out, leaving just an acrid smoke cloud hanging over the mission station. As the inflatables were beached, the priest, Father Damian, came hurrying across to Mr Crown.

'I can't thank you enough!' he exclaimed, putting out his hand.

Mr Crown ignored it. 'What happened?' he snapped.

'Bandits! You're SOS? They knew you were coming, told us not to cooperate with you, set fire to our church as a warning.'

Mr Crown turned to Bailey and Bonsoir. 'Make sure they're gone, then set up a perimeter.'

The two Artists had their automatic weapons ready, and immediately moved out in different directions. Dr Faustus also had his handgun out, but he quickly holstered it.

'You have a doctor?' he asked.

'Dr Leota. He's out touring the villages, but we've called him back.'

Dr Faustus nodded, then moved forward to help the nurses.

The priest said, 'I thought they were going to kill us! I promised we wouldn't help you . . . but you're here

o

now. You can protect us, yes?'

Mr Crown thumbed back at Dr Kincaid. 'Ask him.'

Father Damian hesitated for a moment before rushing up to repeat his thanks to Dr Kincaid, who was altogether more welcoming. Mr Crown strode after Bonsoir and Bailey.

Michael helped Katya pull the boats fully ashore. They picked up bits and pieces of the priest's conversation with Dr Kincaid, at one point hearing the words 'white suit'.

'How did he get here before us?' Michael whispered to Katya.

'He's local. With these rivers, there's probably a thousand shortcuts.'

Michael scanned the rainforest. It began less than thirty metres from where they were standing.

'Do you think he's watching us now?'

'Probably.'

Several workers from the small hospital had suffered smoke inhalation. Two others had been quite badly beaten by the bandits. The priest himself had a bruise forming under one of his eyes. Dr Faustus was respectful of the mission doctor, Dr Leota, when he arrived back, and appreciative of the mission nurses.

There was nothing worse than an outsider blundering in and trying to take over, even if he was more qualified than probably any other doctor on the island.

'Never,' he said to Michael, 'never underestimate the strength of local knowledge. Sure, these guys have been well trained, but nothing in a book is going to tell you how to deal with the insect bites you get out here. Half of them aren't even known to science yet.'

The hospital was a long, low building, with about thirty beds inside. All of them were occupied, half by children, and most were suffering from malaria.

Michael had been taking his malaria pills, and had had a preventative injection, but he knew from Katya that there were dozens of different types of malaria, some relatively mild, some positively lethal, and no amount of medication could protect you against every different strain of it.

Avoiding it, said Dr Faustus, was fifty per cent medicine, and fifty per cent luck.

As they toured the hospital, Dr Leota gave Dr Faustus the rundown on his patients. The single ward was clean and bright, but there was a definite lack of modern equipment and, as Dr Leota lingered over one young boy, a shortage of *primaquine*, *quinine*, *sulphadoxine*, and a whole list of other anti-malarial drugs.

'This kid,' said Dr Leota, 'came in yesterday, barely lucid. We think he has been wandering lost for days. Nobody has claimed him, and if they don't soon it may be too late. I'm not sure he'll last the night.'

As the doctors moved on, Michael looked down at the feverish, starved-looking boy. He was probably about the same age as himself. Michael wondered what his story was, where his family was, or even if he had one. He hadn't the slightest idea how hard it was actually to live in the rainforest. Michael lifted the chart at the foot of the bed; there were notes on it, but he couldn't understand what they said. All he could read was the name at the top.

Michael nodded down at the boy. 'Well, Joe,' he said, 'hope you make it through the night.'

Darkness fell quickly. Instead of pitching the tents Father Damian insisted on them sleeping in the dormitory accommodation which adjoined the church. He also invited them for dinner. He had been priest at St Mark's for five years and was due to be transferred elsewhere in the next few months.

'I love it here,' he said, 'but at the same time I'll be

pleased to go. It's just relentless. The illness, the poverty, the starvation, the violence – and don't get me started on the insects. Everything is always damp. If you set an apple down, the ants carry it off the moment you look away. And the language! Usually when I go to a new posting, I pick the local lingo up straight away. Here they have – and I'm being quite serious – about two hundred different languages. It's impossible!'

Katya leant in to Michael at the table and whispered, 'He says there's poverty and starvation, but he doesn't look like he's been on small portions.'

He was, undoubtedly, very much overweight.

Father Damian glanced up and saw that they were whispering and looking in his direction. He lifted a napkin, dabbed at his sweaty upper lip and said, 'Dr Kincaid, I'm surprised that you've brought children with you on what must be a very dangerous mission.'

Michael and Katya bristled.

Dr Kincaid took his time with his own napkin before saying, 'Michael and Katya are valued members of our team.'

Katya smiled sarcastically at the priest.

Father Damian said, 'Really?' and returned to eating

his dinner. He swallowed one mouthful, and was just shovelling up another, when he paused, set his fork down and looked directly at Dr Kincaid. 'You know, I warned your sister not to go.'

The Artists knew that Dr Roper had set out on her quest from St Mark's, taking with her two trackers, two assistants and enough supplies to keep them all going for a month.

Dr Kincaid nodded. 'Because of the bandits.'

'Yes, but also . . .' He paused then, and his eyes flitted up to the ceiling. 'Because I did not feel that it was God's will for her to go.'

Mr Crown rolled his eyes.

'Really,' said Dr Kincaid. 'Why would you think that?' he asked.

Father Damian clasped his hands before him. 'The people here have been very difficult to convert to Christianity. Even those that do mostly only do it to get easier access to food and medicine. We don't *deny* it to non-believers, but we have to look after our own flock first. But when times are hard, my converts often fall back on their old beliefs, old traditions, the old spirits. I understand that. Lately they have been very unsettled. They believe there are evil spirits at work in the forest.'

'Sure,' said Bailey, 'and one of them's wearing a white suit.'

The Artists smiled among themselves.

Father Damian said, 'Yes, of course. But more than that. There is something in the air, something . . . not quite right.'

'How do you mean?' Katya asked.

'I can't quite put my finger on it. People get restless all the time. Animals generally do not. Because there is a certain amount of waste food here, we tend to get a lot of animal scavengers. Rats, mice, possums, but these last few days, nothing. The birds of paradise always wake me up in the morning with their singing. These past few days – nothing. And then there's the chickens.'

'Chickens?' said Dr Kincaid.

'We keep a lot of chickens. Hundreds of them. These last two days, they haven't laid a single egg between them.'

He raised an eyebrow, and looked around the table.

Dr Kincaid was nodding thoughtfully.

'So what do you think it means?' Bailey asked.

'God only knows,' said Father Damian.

Chapter Seven

This was exactly where Michael didn't want to be.

Yes, when it was first suggested he had been quite excited by the prospect of standing guard from 2 a.m. until 5 a.m. Yes, he had briefly imagined himself as the heroic first line of defence between the bandits and another attack on the mission station. And yes, he quite fancied being equipped with his own assault rifle, a handgun, and a night-vision pocketscope which would allow him to spot enemies approaching in pitch darkness. The reality, however, was . . . just not very exciting. Yes, he had all of those things. But watching rodents scurrying about soon lost its attraction, being plagued by insects made him seek regular shelter behind a mosquito net, and he had exerted himself so much while adventuring around the Arctic that he still hadn't caught up on his sleep, and now he could barely keep his eyes open.

Katya joined him for the early part of his watch. She sprayed him with insect repellent and made sure as little of his skin as possible was exposed. Then she showed him how to use the assault rifle and handgun – without actually firing off any bullets. She paced the perimeter Mr Crown had approved around the mission station with Michael and warned him not to venture beyond it, and then she carefully led him up the rather shaky remains of the small bell tower at the church, which she said was the best position from which to watch the land surrounding three sides of the mission and the river on the fourth.

'If anything happens,' she said, 'ring the bell.'

She then removed the iPod he had brought with him to help him pass the time.

'Concentrate,' she warned him.

And he did, right up to the point where he fell fast asleep. He was *tired*. He was also, he later admitted, *useless*. He couldn't help it. His head fell forward half a dozen times, jolting him awake. He came up with a cunning plan: if he closed his eyes for just five minutes, that would be enough to refresh him and he could then undertake his guard duties with renewed vigour. Except, obviously, the five minutes turned into thirty-five minutes, and he only woke up because his elbow slipped off the outer wall of the bell tower window, causing him to crack his nose on the windowsill. *Then* he was truly awake – and suddenly aware of the creak on the stairs. Someone was coming up and he had no way of knowing if they were friend or foe. Michael fumbled for the assault rifle, raised it, moved to the top of the steps, fingered the trigger and stared through the scope, trying to stop himself from shaking with nerves as the sound moved inexorably closer.

As clarity returned, thoughts raced through his mind as fast as his heartbeat.

How would a bandit know he was in the bell tower?

Because he has night vision as well.

If it was a friend, he or she would just walk up the steps, not sneak up with only little creaks to give him away.

They know I'm the only one awake. If they take me out they can kill everyone else in their sleep.

Shoot first, ask questions later.

Another creak. Closer. Any second, any *moment*.

His heart was going to explode out of his chest.

Shoot! Shoot! Shoot!

His finger pressed down on the trigger. Sweat rolled down his brow.

Shoot! Shoot! Shoot!

I'm going to do it! I'm going to do it! I'm going to—

'Michael? I brought you a cup of coffee, help keep you awake!'

Dr Kincaid. Michael slipped his finger off the trigger and leant the assault rifle against the wall just as the SOS founder rounded the corner.

'Thank you,' said Michael. 'Much appreciated.'

Every item of clothing he had was *stuck* to him. His hair was plastered to his skull. He was trying to gasp for breath, without looking as if he was gasping for breath. His heart was racing so fast that the very last thing he needed was caffeine. Nevertheless he smiled widely and took the cup off Dr Kincaid, cradling it and sipping from it.

I am an idiot and a liability.

'You OK?' Dr Kincaid asked.

'Yeah, fine. You couldn't sleep?'

'Nope. Surprising how quickly your eyes get used to the dark, isn't it? And the insects aren't half as bad when you keep the light off.'

He leant on the sill and looked out across the mission to the forest beyond. He blew air out of his cheeks.

Michael said, 'Your sister.'

'Yep. She's out there somewhere. She's alive, I know she is.'

'Then we'll find her.'

'Yes, we will.' He shook his head and gave a short, sad laugh. 'We never really got on that well. We went our separate ways when we were quite young. Funny how we both ended up trying to save the world. Anyway, I should get back to bed – we've got a long day ahead of us.'

When he'd gone Michael spent the next hour wondering if Dr Kincaid was including Katya and him in that long day – and having waking nightmares about how he had almost shot dead the founder and leader of SOS.

His shift ended just as the first hint of dawn was beginning to appear in the sky. Bailey was taking over. Michael handed over the pocketscope.

'All quiet?' Bailey asked.

'All quiet,' Michael confirmed.

'Then go and catch some zees. Going to be a long day.'

That was the second time – and still no indication what the plans for the junior Artists were.

Michael returned to the dormitory, climbed up on to an empty bunk and slipped into his sleeping bag. Around him some of the others were just starting to stir. Katya mumbled something he couldn't make out. He grunted in response and pulled the bag over his head to block out the growing light. He closed his eyes, and almost instantly fell asleep.

He dreamt about a giant spider. It had bitten into his foot and was trying to drag him out of the bunk and back to its lair.

Michael opened his eyes. Mr Crown had hold of his foot and was dragging him out of his bed.

'Wha . . . what . . . what . . . wha . . . ?'

Mr Crown pulled him off the edge and he fell over a metre to the hard wooden floor. He almost broke his neck.

'Outside!'

Mr Crown stomped out of the dorm.

Michael lay on his back, dazed. He glanced at his watch. He had been asleep for precisely *seven minutes*.

Mr Crown was furious about *something*. He just didn't know what. Given the choice between being dragged out of his bed by Mr Crown or that giant spider, Michael would have chosen the spider every time.

He raised himself. Katya was looking at him.

'What have you done now?' she asked.

'I don't know,' he said, shaking his head. 'But I'm blaming you.'

He headed for the door. As he opened it he was aware of Katya rolling out of her own bed.

Mr Crown was waiting outside. Bailey was standing beside him.

'This way,' Mr Crown snapped and began walking towards the river.

Michael followed. Bailey fell in beside him.

'Have I . . . ?' Michael began. 'Am I . . . ?'

'Yes,' said Bailey.

They came to the river bank. Dr Kincaid was already standing there. Because the sun wasn't fully up, the water behind him looked darker and more threatening than usual.

Dr Kincaid said, 'Michael, were you on guard duty last night?'

'Yes, you know I was, you—'

'I know where you were, Michael, and I know what you were supposed to be doing, what I'm asking is, were you actually doing it?'

'Yes, of course I was.'

'So you can explain this?' He nodded off to his right, where the three inflatables had been stacked and secured. Except they weren't inflated any longer. They were completely flat. The craft on the bottom had a long, very visible tear in it.

Michael was shaking his head. But he *knew*. 'Sorry,' he said quietly.

'What was that?' asked Mr Crown.

'I said, I'm sorry. I must have dozed off . . .'

'You were supposed to be protecting us,' said Dr Kincaid.

'I know.' Michael hung his head.

'We're lucky they were content to vandalize the inflatables. They could have come in and cut all our throats. Bailey?'

The pilot was crouching down beside the craft.

'Hard to say. This bottom one looks like it's done for. The other two might be repairable.'

'OK, see what you can do. Bonsoir?'

Michael turned. The language expert and strategic planner was standing close to the edge of the water, examining the ground. 'I can only see one set of footprints. Could just be a local out to cause trouble, or someone our bandit friends left behind to harass us.'

Dr Kincaid nodded. He took a deep breath, and gave Michael a hard look.

'I had intended taking the pair of you with us, but this changes things. First of all, I have to be able to trust you, and after yesterday with the whirlpool and now this, I'm not sure that I can, or that you even have a future with SOS. And second, even if I wanted to, with one boat definitely out of action, there's no room for either of you. So you will stay here, work with Father Damian, and then I'll decide what to do with you when I come back with my sister. Understood?'

Michael nodded. There was nothing he could say.

But Katya's mouth had dropped open. 'You . . . you . . . you . . . you're leaving me, because of what he's done? How is that fair?'

'It's not,' said Dr Kincaid, 'but someone has to make sure he doesn't get into any more trouble, and we really don't have the room for you now. Sorry, Katya, that's the way it is.'

Michael could feel Katya's eyes burning into him, but he kept his own focused on the ground. He wanted it to open up and swallow him.

He had messed up big time.

He was a loser.

Untrustworthy.

Incapable of doing anything right.

A liability.

He was finished with SOS.

As he stared at the ground, a spider walked over his bare foot.

Chapter Eight

Michael was in the hospital. He wasn't helping Father Damian, or Dr Leota, or one of the nurses. He wasn't checking up on Joe, the comatose boy who had managed to survive the night. He wasn't even avoiding Katya, who had sworn vengeance on him. He was writhing in fevered agony, having been bitten by an unidentified spider.

His reaction to getting bitten had been to go 'Aoow!' and violently kick the spider away. It was a tiny spider. Everyone thought he was trying to distract them from his falling asleep on guard duty. He had not only put their lives of risk, but also jeopardized their mission and, ultimately, the chances of Dr Roper coming out of the rainforest alive. While he hopped around cursing and exclaiming further variations of 'Aoow!' the other Artists ignored him. Bailey and

Bonsoir concentrated on repairing the tears in two of the inflatables. Mr Crown and Dr Kincaid pored over maps with the guides and trackers who would accompany them upriver, while Dr Faustus toured the hospital, distributing welcome medical supplies and helping to inoculate the patients against a whole catalogue of tropical diseases.

Meanwhile, Michael grew feverish. He had cramps in his stomach. His breathing grew laboured. His head was sore. He had a tingling sensation in his foot and his hands. He crawled into his bunk. Katya found him there. He was lying with his head covered and his back to her. She spent about five minutes telling him what a miserable specimen of humanity he was, and how he could go back to his damn boarding school and never darken the world of SOS again. Further infuriated by his lack of reaction, she hovered directly over him and bellowed in his one exposed ear: 'Are you even listening to me?!'

In response, he turned quickly and threw up over the side of the bed, missing her feet by centimetres. Only then did she see the sweat cascading down his brow, and the way his eyes bulged and rolled back in his head. And then she noticed his foot, protruding from the blankets at the bottom, and the fact that it had turned purplish and swollen to twice its normal size.

'Oh! Wait here!'

As if he was going anywhere. She charged out of the dorm, yelling for Dr Faustus.

Late that evening Michael began to emerge from his feverish sleep. Paraffin lamps gave off a dull light in the hospital ward. It took a few minutes for his eyes to focus. He slowly became aware that the shape in the chair beside his bed was Katya. She was asleep.

He stretched. He tried to focus his thoughts. A horrified shudder ran through him as he remembered his humiliation by the river bank. He was angry at himself for falling asleep and letting his comrades down. And then he felt angry *at them*. Hadn't he just survived a near-death experience in the Arctic? Hadn't he just pushed his body to its very limits? He had scarcely had time to recover – all he had managed was a quick doze on the SOS jet. And yet they had expected him to stay up half the night on guard duty. Who did they think they were? He was fourteen, for God's sake. While they had sat back in their Arctic headquarters doing virtually nothing, he had battled bad guys and polar bears, he had recovered the Eden

74

satellite. He was a hero. And his reward? Guarding them while they slept! They had suckered him into thinking it was a great honour to be part of SOS, to go on exciting adventures with the Artists, but the reality surely was that *they* were exploiting *him*. There were laws against that. He should sue them. Dr Kincaid loved to project a positive image of SOS and what it did. How would the founder like it if he revealed how they treated kids? Orphaned kids, at that.

Katya said, 'Are you OK?'

Michael tried to say, 'OK,' but his throat was too dry. She handed him a bottle of water. He drank greedily.

'Turns out you were right to be scared of spiders. Extreme allergic reaction. It doesn't mean it'll happen every time a spider bites you, it was just that particular type, whatever it was. Unfortunately Dr Faustus had to amputate your leg.'

Michael nearly jumped out of his skin. He hurled his bed covers back to reveal . . . two perfectly good and healthy legs. There was a small plaster on his left foot.

'Funny,' he rasped.

'Not as funny as your idea of standing guard.'

He sighed. 'Yeah, well. It doesn't matter any more,

does it? Sooner they send me home the better.'

Katya nodded for several moments. Then she said quietly, 'This is your home.'

'Good point. Leave me in the rainforest. I've really nowhere else to go.'

'I mean, SOS. They're not just going to throw you out. Dr Kincaid said so.'

'Did he? When?'

'When you were thrashing about in a fever and Dr Faustus said you would probably die and Dr Leota said you probably wouldn't, and Mr Crown said you were an idiot, and Bailey said you were exhausted and shouldn't have been on duty, and Dr Kincaid said that was a good point, he was focused on other things and should have realized, and Mr Crown said you were an idiot again, and Bonsoir said you made good coffee and Dr Faustus said you saved our hides because we made a big fuss about how we were going to find the Eden satellite and we would have looked like fools, but you found it, and Dr Kincaid said that was a good point and Mr Crown said you were still an idiot and Bailey said he hoped you didn't die because you'd the makings of a good Artist, and Dr Faustus agreed, and Bonsoir agreed and Dr Kincaid agreed and Mr Crown said he didn't think your coffee was that good.'

Michael was trying to take all of it in. Finally he said, 'What about you?'

'What about me?'

'What did you say about me?'

'Me? They didn't ask me.'

'And if they had?'

'I would have pointed out that you didn't save the Eden by yourself. Anyway, enough of bigging you up, do you want something to eat?'

'Yes. No. Maybe. Where are they all? The Artists?'

'Gone.'

'Oh.'

'They couldn't wait. Dr Leota assured them you would be OK. So they went. They have to save Dr Roper.'

'I know. I'm sorry.'

'I know you are.'

'Really, I am.'

'Don't worry. You'll pay for it.'

She left him to sleep. Predictably, he dreamt about spiders. And having one leg. He woke, drenched in sweat, in the early hours of the morning. He drained another bottle of water. He went to the bathroom. It stank. He knew he was spoiled by western living.

Michael dragged his weary carcass back down the ward. He paused at Joe's bed. The boy was behind a mosquito net. He lifted his chart and studied it. He was just turning away when Joe spoke. His voice was weak, and in a language Michael didn't recognize. This was hardly surprising. Bonsoir had said it was the most linguistically diverse area in the world.

Michael's response was just to shrug and say, 'Sorry, no speako,' like the idiot he knew he was.

The boy surprised him by responding immediately with, 'English?'

'Yes . . . you speak English?'

'Where . . . where am I?'

'St Mark's Mission Station.'

Joe shook his head vaguely. 'I don't . . . who are you?'

'Michael. I'm . . .' He didn't know what to say. Was he with SOS, or the Artists? Or was he just an orphan stuck in a rainforest on the wrong side of the world? 'I . . . was bitten by a spider. You OK?'

Joe touched his arms, then threw back his covers and ran his hands along his legs and torso. He nodded. 'How long have I been here?'

'I'm not sure. I've only just arrived. Your English is very good.'

'My father, he was educated in Australia. I don't remember . . . what is wrong with me?'

'I don't know . . . but I'm afraid they had to amputate your leg.'

Joe looked horrified. He whipped off his blanket and saw two perfectly good legs. He looked at Michael. 'I have two legs.'

'Yes, so it would appear.'

'Why did you say I had a leg amputated?'

'I . . . was only joking.'

Joe looked utterly confused. 'Why would you make a joke of that?'

'I . . . just . . .'

'You think it is funny to lose a leg?'

'No, I . . . sorry, I didn't, I was thinking of someone else.'

'Someone else has lost a leg?'

'Yes. No. Maybe. I've had a fever, I should lie down.'

Joe was feeling his legs. 'Is there something wrong with them? Are they going to cut one of them off? I do not see injuries. Why would . . . ?'

'Look, someone should know that you're awake. They can tell you everything, I'm sure. Just wait, I'll go and get Dr Leota or one of the nurses.'

Michael turned. But as he crossed the ward he staggered suddenly to one side. Maybe he'd got up too soon. He was weaker than he thought. It felt like the whole world was moving.

And then he realized the whole world *was* moving.

The ground beneath him was shuddering.

Medical equipment shook and toppled over.

Patients were waking up all around him, terrified and screaming.

Behind him a paraffin lamp teetered perilously on the edge of a windowsill before falling and bursting into flames.

There was only one word for it:

Earthquake!

Chapter Nine

'*No*. It was not an earthquake,' said Katya. She was quite adamant.

'The ground shook. It quaked. Therefore it was an earthquake.'

'It was a tremor. They happen all the time in this part of the world. The tectonic plates rub together and—'

'I don't need to know the science. By anyone's standards it was an earthquake, just admit it.'

'It was a small, tiny tremor, nothing to worry about.'

'The hospital nearly burned down!'

'It did not. The fire was put out very quickly. It was a tremor. Buildings that are not very well built will obviously suffer the greatest damage, but there's hardly a scratch on the hospital and a good puff of wind would probably blow it over. A lamp was placed too close to the edge of a windowsill and it fell, that's all. Relax. It was a minor tremor.'

'It was an earthquake.'

They were not destined to agree on *anything*, *ever*. Michael just knew what he had felt under his feet, and the terror it had inspired in his fellow patients. It was an earthquake. Yes, the fire had been put out very quickly, and there was no real damage, but it didn't change the fact of what he had experienced.

Dr Leota, much to Michael's chagrin, agreed with Katya. As he gave Michael the once-over, he said that the tremors had been coming with increasing frequency.

'However, I studied in England,' he said, 'and when it rains there you exaggerate everything, you say words like *downpour* and *torrential*. When it is windy you say it is *blowing a gale*. If you had felt that tremor in London, it would have been a *major earthquake*. But you do not really know what the forces of nature are capable of. You want wind and floods? Spend the rainy season here, my friend, spend it here.'

'He might yet,' said Katya, who was sitting on the bed beside Michael. She gave him a sarcastic wink.

Dr Leota moved to Joe's bed. The boy was hungry, thirsty, covered in insect bites and generally traumatized. He could hardly remember what had happened to him, where he was from or how he had come to be wandering in the rainforest. Dr Leota listened to his chest, then asked Joe to lean forward so that he could examine his back.

'Seem to be healing nicely,' he said after a few moments. 'You still don't know how you got these?'

Joe shook his head. Michael peered around him on one side, Katya on the other. Katya immediately made a face. 'Burns?' she asked.

Dr Leota nodded. 'Really very severe. Fortunately he received some rudimentary treatment for them before he got here. I don't know if they were caused by an accident or were done deliberately. Unfortunately neither does he.'

'You mean like torture?' Michael asked.

'Torture. Punishment. There are no laws out here, at least not as you would know them.'

'How do you mean?' Michael asked.

'He means tribal law,' said Katya, 'traditional law, going back thousands of years.'

'Here on New Ireland, in some of the more remote villages,' said Dr Leota, 'there's a secret society, the Duk-Duk, which represents a rough sort of law and order. The problem with it is that because there's nothing written, it's all handed down, so it's often open to misinterpretation, if you're feeling charitable, or corruption, if you're not. These burns could be a punishment or—'

But Joe was shaking his head. 'No. It was not Duk-Duk. It was . . . raining fire . . .'

Michael looked at Katya and raised an eyebrow. He was thinking: *more like raining rocks, and one hit you on the head.*

Obviously, he didn't *say* that.

But they were all looking at him. So obviously he *had* said it out loud.

'I just mean . . .' Michael shrugged, then rapidly tried to change the subject. 'When I spoke to you before the *earthquake*, you said you learnt English from your father, that he was taught it in Australia – so you must remember something . . . ?'

'My father . . . Australia . . .' Joe's eyes began to dart about as he desperately tried to grasp his memories.

Dr Leota patted his hand reassuringly. 'Don't worry about it,' he said calmly. 'You have been through a traumatic experience – your mind and body are in shock. You need to rest, get some more sleep. Your memories will come back to you soon enough.'

Dr Leota smiled and got up. When he left the ward, Michael and Katya went with him. He stood in the yard outside, his face up to the sun.

'*Will* his memories come back?' Katya asked.

Dr Leota gave a vague kind of a nod. 'I don't know. It's quite possible he's suffered some kind of brain trauma. Problem is, out here, I don't have access to a CAT scan, so I can't check for injury. There are no *obvious* signs of brain damage, but sometimes you just don't know.'

'Well, shouldn't you take him somewhere where you can check?' Michael asked.

Dr Leota smiled.

'What?' asked Michael.

'We're not in England now, Michael,' said Katya. 'It's not as simple as that.'

'Katya's right. It's just not practical. He's talking, he walked out of the hospital just fine when we had the quake, I'm sure he's OK.'

He began to walk towards the treatment centre, where a line of locals had already formed, stretching along the facing wall and disappearing around the corner. Dr Leota stopped and looked back at them. 'Well?'

'Well what?' asked Michael.

'You're supposed to be helping. Mr Crown made it very clear before he left: remember, he said, they're not on holiday, they're here to work.'

Michael took a deep breath. He was not *at all* surprised.

There was Dr Leota and three nurses. And then there was a line of patients that seemed to grow and grow and grow. They emerged from the forest, they floated upriver on leaky boats, they pedalled along deeply rutted tracks on rickety bicycles or clung perilously to gasping, belching motor scooters. They had infected cuts and swelling eyes and wracking coughs and broken bones. They had burns, and worms, and malaria. They had every kind of ailment Michael could imagine, and many he couldn't. Katya was already efficient at delivering inoculations, so she took charge of a line of children and their mothers, giving injections against a whole range of diseases in one arm-numbing shot. Michael helped change dressings and quickly learnt the art of applying plaster casts to broken bones. He did a lot of fetching and carrying.

They took twenty minutes for lunch, flopping down in the yard outside, enjoying the sun. They ate freshly cooked fish. Katya's vegetarianism wasn't mentioned.

In the afternoon, by which time the queue outside the treatment centre was down to a more manageable size, Father Damian brought them both across to the school. There were around sixty pupils, ranging in age from five to fifteen, all in the one class and with the priest himself as their teacher. There was a large map of the world pinned to one wall, and an old-fashioned blackboard. No computers, no calculators, and desks that came in a dozen different sizes and styles.

Before they entered the classroom they stood outside the glassless window and listened as Father Damian led his pupils in a hymn.

Katya nudged Michael. 'Look at their uniforms.'

'What about them?'

'Everything is so basic around here. Their homes don't have running water or electricity, but their uniforms are so bright and clean. Look at their shirts.' Their white shirts were pristine. 'They're clean because they make sure they're kept that way. They don't have much, but they appreciate that they're getting an education. Their way of saying thank you is quite simple: they keep themselves neat and tidy.'

Michael shook his head. 'You are *so* patronizing,' he said, and slipped inside before she could thump him.

* * *

It was an enjoyable but exhausting afternoon. Father Damian taught in a mixture of English and local words and phrases he had picked up. Somehow it all made sense. After a while Joe slipped into the back of the classroom and sat against the rear wall. Katya told them all about SOS, and Michael made fun of her. Then Michael related their adventures in the Arctic, and Katya made rude hand signals behind his back. Father Damian pretended to get angry. Everyone was laughing.

Later, out in the yard, the kids streamed past, smiling. Several gathered round Michael and Katya, hurling rapid-fire questions at them. They showed no inclination to go home at all, at least until Father Damian came up and sent them on their way. When they had dispersed Michael saw Joe sitting by himself on the grass. As he approached he saw that the boy had tears on his cheeks. He didn't know whether to check he was OK or leave him to his thoughts.

Before he could decide, he was distracted by Katya talking on her satellite phone. He followed her as she sauntered towards the river. She became aware of him shadowing her, and waved him away, but he stayed right there with her. When she was finished she cut the line, put the phone away, and then fixed him with a deadly look.

'Ever think of giving someone a bit of privacy?' she snapped.

'No,' said Michael. 'What's happening?'

'Nothing's happening.'

'Have they found her?'

'No.'

'Have they found any trace of her?'

'No.'

'Have they been attacked by cannibals and eaten?'

'Yes.'

'Yes?'

'No. Idiot.'

She walked off.

That night they lay in their beds looking through the open window at the white-brick hospital building. They had helped Dr Leota for several hours after dinner, but then he said they'd done everything they could and told them to go get a good night's sleep. They had presumed that he was finished as well. But no, he was clearly visible in the lamplight, going from bed to bed checking on his patients.

'He works hard,' said Katya.

'Too hard,' said Michael.

'What choice does he have? He's the only doctor for miles.'

Michael nodded in the darkness. 'Speaking of which?'

'What?'

'The other doctor in our lives? Dr Kincaid? Are you going to tell me now what he had to say?'

'Say please.'

Michael sighed.

'Say please,' Katya repeated.

'Please.'

'Say please tell me what—'

'Just forget it! I'm not interested!'

Katya giggled. 'Michael Monroe. You are *so easy* to wind up. If you must know, no, there's nothing to report. They were just setting camp for the night, about forty miles upriver. No sign of Dr Roper.'

'What about bandits?'

'Nope, nothing from them either.'

'So they've nothing to report.'

'Nope. Apart from . . .'

'Yes . . . ?'

'Spiders as big as your fist.'

In the darkness, Michael swallowed.

Chapter Ten

Michael sat bolt upright in the half light of dawn, bathed in sweat and clawing at his face, convinced there was a huge spider on it. He had definitely heard it, its feet tap-tap-tapping along the windowsill towards him; he knew *most* spiders didn't make that much noise, but this one was wearing boots.

No – that couldn't be right.

He tried to shake the fog out of his head. Spiders in boots! But he could still hear that tap-tap-tapping. He peered into the gloom. With the departure of the Artists the dormitory was empty but for himself and Katya. She had drawn a curtain around her bed to give her a little privacy, and it was from beyond it that the tap-tap-tapping was definitely coming.

Michael threw back his sheets and leant across. He pulled the edge of the curtain up.

Katya was sitting on top of her bed, her laptop open and tap-tap-tapping away, at least until she broke off to glare at him. 'Yes?'

'Sorry. You woke me up with your typing. What are you doing?'

She closed the laptop. 'Thinking.'

'About . . . ?'

Katya rolled off the bed. 'We need to talk to Joe.'

'Joe? What—?'

'You'll find out.'

She lifted her laptop and strode towards the door.

'Katya.' She ignored him. She pulled the door open. 'Katya!'

'*What?!*'

'Maybe you should put some clothes on?'

She wasn't *naked*, but she was in a flimsy T-shirt and knickers. 'Close your eyes!' she shouted and dived back behind her curtain.

Two minutes later, and with her red face only starting to fade, she was marching across the dusty yard towards the hospital, with Michael hurrying along beside her firing questions, which she resolutely ignored.

Patients were just beginning to stir as they entered the ward. Joe, however, was still fast asleep. At least until Katya jabbed his shoulder and said, 'Joe. Joe. Joe. Joe. Joe. Joe.'

He sat up suddenly, panic-stricken, already starting to climb out of bed. Katya put the flat of her palm on his chest to stop him.

'It's OK,' she said. 'I just need to ask you something.'

Joe took a deep breath, then rested back on his pillow.

'When we spoke to you yesterday, you said it was raining fire.'

Joe closed his eyes, thinking for a moment, before nodding.

'Tell me what you meant.'

'I meant . . . it was raining fire. Burning rocks were landing all around us and exploding.'

'Us?' said Michael.

'Shhh,' said Katya. 'What do you mean *us*?'

Michael could see Joe's eyes moving behind his closed lids. It was as if his memories were all stored in a room, and he managed to force the door open just enough for a little chink of light to escape.

'I . . . was running . . . I was being chased . . . men, men with guns . . . I was running for hours and hours . . .'

'Why were they chasing you?'

'I don't remember . . .'

'Why were they chasing you?'

Katya's voice was harsh, demanding. Michael's eyes snapped up to her. Heads swivelled from other beds.

'I don't remember!'

'You do! Just *tell us*!'

'No! I don't remem—'

'Tell us! Why were they chasing you, why did they have guns, who were they, Joe? Why were they chasing you?'

'Because they wanted to kill me!'

'Why?'

'Because they killed my father!'

With that his eyes opened, and tears sprang.

Katya put her hand to her mouth. 'I'm sorry, Joe, I didn't mean . . .'

'No. It's OK.' He dragged a hand across his face. 'I . . . it has come back . . . I remember . . . I remember . . .' He looked suddenly shocked. His voice dropped. He sniffed up. He nodded to himself. 'My father . . . they killed him. The bandits . . . they came to our village and shot him, and then they came back and tried to kill me . . .'

Michael sat on the edge of his bed. 'Why, Joe?'

Joe's brow furrowed as he grasped for the facts, and then when he spoke again it was as if someone was turning a tap on, and the words began to spring out of him, faster and faster. 'Land . . . they wanted our land, and my father was chief . . . and he said no . . . and they murdered him. And the people . . . didn't want to sell, but they were scared of the bandits, so they thought that because I was so young, that they would make me chief, and I would agree to sell, and they wouldn't feel so bad about what they had done because it was my decision. But I refused, because I knew my father would never sell. So the bandits burned our village, and they tried to kill me, and they chased me into the forest. They wouldn't give up, I ran and I ran and I ran, but still they came.'

'And the rest of your family?' Michael asked.

Joe shook his head. 'My mother – I don't know. I think she was killed also.'

'What's your village called?' Katya asked.

'Kono. If it is still there.'

Katya snapped her laptop open and tapped rapidly. Then she swung it round for Joe to see and pointed at the Google map of New Ireland she'd pulled up.

'This is it, Joe, see? Now what direction did you run in?'

He peered in at the map. 'Direction? I'm not sure . . .'

'Inland, yes?'

'Yes.'

'Towards these mountains?'

'Yes?'

'Which one?'

Joe looked confused. 'What do you mean?'

'This is the Hans Meyer Range, it runs right down the middle of your island. It would be helpful to know which of them you ran towards.'

'Why?' Michael asked.

'Just bear with me, would you? Joe?'

'It was the tallest mountain.'

'This one? Mount Taron.'

'I think, yes.'

'And this was where it rained fire?'

'I think . . . it is like a nightmare. I can remember . . . burning . . . and then . . . I am not so sure . . . but it will come back, I'm sure it will. I just remember being so tired . . . and wanting to lie down and . . .'

Katya patted his hand. 'It's OK, Joe. That's all I need. You've been great. You go back to sleep for a while, OK? Do you want something to drink?'

Joe nodded his head vaguely. His mind was far

away – reliving.

Katya looked at Michael. 'Get him some water.'

'Do I look like your servant?'

Katya thought about that for just a moment. 'Yes,' she said.

At first Michael couldn't find Katya. It had taken him a few minutes to track down a bottle of water for Joe, and when he emerged from the hospital again there was no sign of her.

Though it was still early St Mark's was already busy. Builders were working on the fire-damaged sections of the church. The first children were beginning to arrive for school, chirping happily. Dr Leota walked along the line already starting to form outside the treatment centre, smiling and chatting, but actually on his way to the hospital to check on his patients first. Michael peered into the school, and the church, and then walked the perimeter of the mission station looking for her. He lingered by the damaged inflatable, shaking his head at his own stupidity, and then slowly made his way back to the dorm, where he finally found her pacing up and down muttering to herself.

Michael stood in the doorway, arms folded. 'What is it now?'

'I'm so stupid,' said Katya.

'I know that.'

'Why didn't I see it?'

'Because you're so stupid?' She ignored him and kept pacing. 'See what?'

'It! What do you think?'

'I don't know, but if you'd care to—'

'It was the chickens!'

'What chickens?'

'Not the chickens! The hens! Their eggs!'

'What about them?'

'Don't you listen? Father Damian said. They haven't been laying their eggs.'

'So . . . *what* . . . ?'

Katya stopped dead. 'Oh, you moron. Listen to me. Why would chickens stop laying eggs?'

'I don't *know*.'

'It's a well-known fact that animals behave unusually in the run-up to natural disasters.'

'Is it?'

'Yes! Birds fly south, cows stop giving milk and chickens stop laying!'

'I'll take your word for it.'

'OK! It's not exactly scientifically proven, but it *happens*, believe me. But then the earth tremor—'

'Quake . . .'

'Listen to me! It's a classic early warning sign! The eggs, the tremor, fireballs from the mountain . . . it's not an earthquake we have to worry about. It's a volcano!'

Chapter Eleven

'Over here!'

Dr Kincaid acknowledged the tracker and quickly picked up his pace. They had been marching, climbing, cutting and sliding their way through the rainforest for six hours; they were all soaked and exhausted and stung and bitten and bruised. Nobody complained. They had the best and the latest and the most expensive hi-tech equipment in the world; they could, conceivably, have remained in their headquarters back in England and carried out ninety per cent of the search just as efficiently from the comfort of their nice leather office chairs, drinking cappuccinos while they studied satellite photos and thermal images and monitoring radio and mobile phone traffic in a hundred different languages, but it was that missing ten per cent that they could never hope to replicate on a computer screen, the ten per cent that was hands on, that got you dirty, that risked your life. The ten per cent that gave them this:

'What is it?' Dr Kincaid asked as he finally caught up with Tracker Mark.

Mark wasn't his real name, but the one Father Damian had given him when he'd baptized him in the camp an hour before they left. Mark probably hadn't even known that he was being baptized, but nodded and smiled through the very short service because he was being well paid for his tracking skills, and even he was aware that none of the SOS team could pronounce his real name. So they called him Mark, after the Disciple.

Mark was holding something up. Something familiar.

As Bonsoir, Dr Faustus, Bailey and Mr Crown hurried up they found Dr Kincaid smiling.

'My sister is very careful about leaving whatever remote part of the world she is visiting in as pristine a condition as when she found it,' he said. 'However, there is no escaping one fact. She has always had a very sweet tooth.'

He held up what Tracker Mark had discovered.

'A Twix wrapper?' said Bailey. 'I could murder one of those right now.'

Bonsoir took it off him, using just the very tips of his fingers. 'I can swipe it for DNA and prints,' he said, 'make sure it's hers.'

'Where else are you going get a Twix out here, unless she brought it?' asked Bailey.

Bonsoir peered inside the wrapper. 'There's no chocolate residue inside. With the heat out here, you would expect there to be some melting, but this is completely clean. So either she had some way of keeping it refrigerated, or there was residue and it has been picked clean by insects.'

Mr Crown shook his head. 'I can't believe we're getting this excited by a Twix wrapper. We *know* she came this way already.'

'No,' said Bonsoir, 'we know her group passed this way, but not necessarily that she was with them. This is direct evidence that she was.'

'Unless,' said Bailey, 'someone stole her Twix.'

Mr Crown rolled his eyes. 'Let's just get moving.'

He led the way. Bonsoir and Bailey grinned at each other. They enjoyed winding Crown up.

They pushed on for another sweltering hour before stopping to rest, eat and to allow Dr Kincaid to make contact with HQ in England. They might have been in an extremely remote location, but he was still the leader of SOS, and responsible for its activities in half a dozen different parts of the world. While the others checked equipment and cooked, Dr Kincaid gave interviews via webcam, talked to fundraisers, and addressed volunteers on three continents. Nobody he spoke to could have guessed that his sister was missing or how worried he was about her.

When he had finished, Bonsoir brought him food, and then crouched down at his side, looking grim-faced.

'Tell,' Dr Kincaid said simply.

'Been speaking to Katya and Michael.'

'What have they done now?'

'Done? Oh – nothing. Not that I know of anyway. It's what they're saying.'

Dr Kincaid knew that Bonsoir wouldn't have bothered to relate Katya's theory about the volcano if he didn't think there was something to it. So he listened attentively, ignored his food, and felt a kernel of fear begin to grow and blossom as Bonsoir described the possibilities.

'Problem is, volcanoes have been poked and prodded by scientists for the past hundred years, but we still can't really tell exactly what sets them off or predict if they're going to blow big time. Mount Taron has been dormant for ten thousand years, but if it is suddenly active again, well, it could go a couple of different ways – either it will collapse in on itself and simmer down, or it could explode, send out superheated gases and lava that will destroy everything in its path and quite possibly bury this entire island. Or could be something in between the two. We just don't know.'

'And there's been no whispers about this?'

'Nothing. All volcanoes thought to be at risk are routinely monitored. Either Mount Taron isn't considered one, or someone somewhere is misreading the signs.'

'Katya's no expert on volcanoes.'

'Nope. But it's better to be safe than sorry. Equally we don't want to start a panic. I think we should take a look ourselves. We get back to Put Put, take up the chopper and get as close as we can. We can relay images back to HQ, get a proper analysis and then if there is a problem we can release the word and get our evacuation procedures underway.'

Dr Kincaid was nodding. 'OK, you take Bailey with you and get back to Put Put.'

'You . . . ?'

'I'll press on with the others until we find my sister.'

Bonsoir gave him a long look. 'If this thing blows, we're going to need you. Governments listen to you, not the rest of us. We can't have you in the middle of nowhere, maybe unable to get a signal. This is why you set SOS up.'

'I know that. I'll be there when I'm needed. But for now we press on.'

Bonsoir nodded. He was the boss. 'What'll I tell Katya?' he asked.

'Tell her well done.'

'Will I pick them up on the way past, get them out of the danger zone?'

Dr Kincaid nodded slowly. He was staring out into the forest, lost in his own thoughts. 'Yes, get them out of there. I have one sister missing and in danger, I don't need the rest of my family at risk.'

Bonsoir began to turn away, but then hesitated. 'You mean we're all one big family, right?'

But Dr Kincaid was no longer listening.

Chapter Twelve

'I don't know what you're so annoyed about,' Katya was saying. 'The logical thing is to get back to Put Put, find out what we can about the volcano, then if it's bad news, help organize things. We're really not doing anything useful here. Anyway, I thought you'd be relieved to get away from the spiders.'

They were standing by the edge of the river. The air was hot and clammy and the flies were buzzing around them. Somehow, they weren't annoying Michael as much as before.

He turned to Katya. 'Did you ever hear the expression, *like rats leaving a sinking ship?*'

'Yes, of course, but we're not . . .'

'First hint of danger, he whips us out of here.'

'We don't know that. In fact, if anything it's going to put us in more danger. Isn't Bailey going to fly over the volcano? If half of them are staying out there looking for Dr Roper, then they're going to need help on the chopper.'

'You think?'

'We'll insist. We're pretty good at that.'

Michael looked back at the mission station. 'We haven't even told them why we're going.'

'We were told not to. It might be nothing.'

'If it was nothing they wouldn't be flying us out. So we *are* deserting them. Dr Leota, Joe and everyone in the hospital, all the kids in the school.'

'Michael, I know what you're saying, but there is no danger just yet. Much better to get back to headquarters and help there, help everyone deal with this, if it happens.'

'It just feels . . . *wrong.*'

She punched him playfully on the arm. 'It'll be fine. Come on. Bailey won't be here for hours yet, we should give Dr Leota a hand while we can and then get packed up.'

Katya began to walk back towards the hospital. Michael hesitated. He had an instinct for things. He knew he had. And every fibre of his being was telling him that leaving the mission station was a mistake. A sudden movement at his feet caught his attention. A spider. A big one. Exactly like the one that had bitten him and almost sent him into a coma. He stood frozen to the spot as it crawled right up on to his foot.

'Come on!' Katya shouted back.

After what felt like an eternity the spider calmly crawled off his foot and back on to the muddy embankment. When he looked closer, it wasn't alone. There were half a dozen others, all walking in the same direction. Downriver.

It probably didn't mean anything.

The next hour passed helping with the mundane but necessary work that a hospital requires every day, every hour and every minute in order to keep it functioning. Cleanliness was the big thing. Insects. Fighting infection. Bandages had to be changed more regularly than in a temperate climate. Heat meant that bacteria multiplied quickly and easily. This meant that more medicine was required than at home, but less was available. It was the Third World. It was the way of life. And death.

As they worked, singing drifted across from the school; a cool breeze helped to lift some of the mugginess. Michael tried to lose himself in what he was doing and enjoy the fact that here he was on the other side of the world, experiencing things he could never have hoped to experience just a few days ago. But every few minutes his idyllic vision of his new life flipped: he saw the mission station in flames, clouds of poisonous gas drifting through the hospital; streams of burning lava trapping the children in their classroom, screaming, and screaming and—

'Michael?'

His head snapped round. He had just been stripping a bed and was standing lost in his thoughts with the sheets in his hand. Joe was smiling at him. Dressed now, in donated clothes. He had on a sky-blue T-shirt with *Manchester City For Ever* written across it.

'Hey, Joe, you OK?'

'Yes. OK. Dr Leota says I am free to go.'

'Go where? Back to your village?' Joe nodded. 'What if the bandits are waiting for you?'

'I have nowhere else to go.'

'How're you going to get there? It's about forty K.'

'I will find a way.'

Katya came up beside them.

Michael said, 'Joe's going. Home.'

She immediately looked concerned. 'But I thought . . . ?'

'I have to find out,' said Joe.

'You should wait,' said Michael. 'Maybe we could drop you back there, make sure it's OK.' He glanced at Katya. She was shaking her head. 'Why not?'

She ignored him. 'I'm sorry, Joe,' she said, 'I hope it turns out all right.'

Katya gave him a hug. Michael just nodded. Joe walked out of the hospital.

Michael immediately snapped, '*Why* can't we help him?'

'Because his village is nowhere near where we're going.'

'We could make a detour.'

'No.'

'Because of the volcano? We don't even know if it's—'

'No, not the volcano. Because we *can't*, Michael.'

'Why *not*?'

'Because there are hundreds of kids like Joe, lost or displaced or homeless or orphaned. We can't help them all.'

'I'm not asking to help them *all*, I'm asking to help one.'

'And ignore all of the others? Joe is well again, he has to make his own way. I know it seems hard, but SOS exists to help in *emergencies*. We are a rapid response organization. We can't put our energies into one boy when there's a bigger picture we have to deal with.'

She turned away.

'Then why are we looking for Dr Roper? She's one person.'

Katya hesitated for a moment before she turned round. 'Because the work she is doing might save the rainforest here, and saving the rainforest here might save it elsewhere, and eventually contribute to the recovery of this planet we've been poisoning for like . . . *ever*.'

'So we would do the same for every environmental scientist who goes missing? Fly halfway around the world, risk our lives for every scientist who gets lost looking for rare monkeys?'

'I . . .' For a moment, just a moment, it looked as if Katya might have been lost for words. Then she shook her head and said, 'You're wrong.'

'How?' he challenged.

'There are no monkeys on New Ireland.'

Katya gave him a sarcastic smile and hurried out of the ward, fully aware that she hadn't answered the question.

Chapter Thirteen

Michael was just finishing packing his rucksack when Katya appeared in the doorway and said, 'Relax, we're going nowhere. At least not yet.'

Bailey had called to say that the seal over the tear in the skin of their inflatable had ruptured, causing water to leak into the engine, which had now failed. They were going to have to stop, carry out repairs, and then give both the engine and the skin time to dry out. That would mean camping out overnight. It would probably be late the following morning before they made it back to St Mark's. Michael couldn't help feeling a twinge of guilt.

At dinner time they sat at the trestle table with Father Damian, Dr Leota and the nurses. There were sweet potatoes, rice and pork laid out before them. Father Damian said grace, and took a long time over it. He thanked God for many, many things.

When he had finished Michael clasped his hands before him and said, 'And thank you for the volcano, which is about to blow.'

Katya glared at him.

Father Damian, who liked his food, was already reaching for it. 'What's that?' he asked as he began to shovel an unhealthy-sized portion on to his plate. 'Volcano? Where? What part of the world are we talking about?'

'Here,' said Michael.

'Here? You mean New Guinea? Yes, it's quite a volatile—'

'He means *here*,' Katya interrupted. 'Mount Taron.'

Father Damian stopped just as he was about to fill his face. His eyes flitted briefly in the direction of the mountain. '*Our* Mount . . . ?' He laughed dismissively. 'How could you possibly know that? I'm sure we would have heard.'

'It's not official,' said Katya. 'But there is evidence emerging.'

'Like what?' He was chewing now, with far too much food in his round face. As he spoke, little pieces of rice flew out. 'What sort of evidence?'

'We have reports of flaming rocks shooting out

of the mountain. The earth tremors you've been experiencing. Even the chickens failing to lay.'

Father Damian swallowed what he had in his mouth, and began to push more on to his fork. There was sweat on his brow. 'Chickens? Yes, indeed, they have stopped laying. The problem with chickens is that they tend to take any excuse they can to stop producing. A car horn, a door closing too loudly. They're extremely temperamental. Your earth tremors – well, they're just a fact of life in this part of the world. As for – what did you say, *flaming* rocks? On the word of one traumatized boy who has been starved and lost and was hallucinating wildly when he was finally brought here?'

'He was *burned*,' said Michael.

'Yes, and I'm afraid that in the absence of electricity in these remote parts of this island, *fire* is what keeps people warm, what many cook on, and it also causes the lion's share of accidents and injuries. Isn't that right, Dr Leota?'

The doctor had not yet begun to eat. 'Father Damian does have a point. Burns take up a lot of our time. However, I wouldn't immediately reject your concerns.'

'Nonsense!' the priest exploded. 'Utter nonsense! Believe me, if there was a volcano about to erupt, there'd be more evidence than lazy chickens and a few minor burns!'

Katya shrugged. 'Well, all I can say is that Dr Kincaid and SOS are taking it seriously enough, and they—'

'*We . . .*' interjected Michael.

'*We* have an excellent track record. I'm presuming you do have an evacuation plan, just in case? It doesn't have to be for the volcano either, it could be for the river flooding, or a full-scale earthquake. You do have the means to get your patients and the schoolkids out if the worst happens?'

'My dear girl,' said Father Damian as he shovelled in some more food. 'We absolutely are not going anywhere. Be it fire or flood or earthquake, we are staying right here. The Good Lord will protect us.'

Michael said, 'What if he's busy?'

Father Damian glared at him. Dr Leota tried to hide his smile. And Katya just pushed her plate away and got up. 'I've lost my appetite,' she said, before stalking off.

'That man,' Katya said later, lying in bed, 'is an idiot.'

'Mmmm,' said Michael.

'What do you mean, *mmm*? There's no doubt about it.'

'He's religious. He believes in all that stuff. If he was a priest and he didn't believe it, he'd be a bit of a hypocrite.'

'Well, he's in charge of the mission, and he's putting everyone's lives at risk. And no doubt when it comes to it he'll have a boat standing by to race him away and he'll leave everyone else behind.'

'Katya, you don't know that.'

She growled.

The breeze had gone and it had grown hotter and stickier, so even with their covers thrown back they found it hard to sleep. Michael was eventually drifting off in the early hours when he became vaguely aware of shouting somewhere in the distance, and then a gunshot, which brought him fully awake in an *instant*. Katya was up just as quickly.

'Bandits?' she hissed in the darkness.

They threw on their clothes as quickly as they could. Katya grabbed her flashlight. Father Damian was just passing as they opened the dorm door.

'What's . . . ?' Katya began.

But he ignored her and hurried on.

'Don't worry,' said Michael, 'God will protect us.'

They emerged into the yard outside. Lights had come on in the hospital. They could see Dr Leota pulling on a pair of boots as he emerged from his own quarters behind the treatment centre. Father Damian was leading them all towards the river when one of the locals he employed came hurrying towards him, talking excitedly.

Father Damian held up his hands to the man and said, 'Slower!'

The man did not appear to slow down at all. But after a few moments the priest turned back to Michael, Katya and Dr Leota and said, 'Nothing to worry about! It's just a local boat. One of the guards was a little bit jumpy and shot at it.'

While Father Damian and the guard conversed with Dr Leota, who had a better understanding of the language, Michael and Katya approached the sloping stretch of river bank and saw that the boat's pilot was just pulling it up on to the sandy incline. Another smaller figure jumped out of it and splashed down into the last few centimetres of water.

'Joe!' Michael exclaimed. 'We thought you'd gone!'

The boy hurried up to them, smiling widely. 'I came back,' he said, 'I came back because I remembered more.'

'Well, that's . . .'

'The doctor! The lady doctor! She treat my wounds! Dr Roper!'

Chapter Fourteen

It took a while to get Joe calmed down. He excitedly spat out what he had to say – but mostly in his own language, the rest in English. They shepherded him back to the canteen, organized some food as he hadn't eaten since leaving the mission station, and then gathered around him at the trestle table in the light of a single paraffin lamp. Father Damian appeared from the kitchen with his own plate.

'It just came back, sudden,' said Joe, breathing easier. 'Thirty kilometres downriver, one minute, nothing . . . the next I remember her.'

'You're sure it was her?' Katya asked. She had her laptop out and spun it round so that he could see the photograph of Dr Kincaid's missing sister she'd pulled up.

Joe nodded enthusiastically. 'That is her.'

'Tell us again,' said Dr Leota, 'only slower.'

'The fire on the mountain, OK? Raining down, OK? The bandits ran, I ran . . . but I got hit . . . I was burning . . . rolling over . . . and then I . . . lights out?'

'Blacked out,' said Katya.

'Yes, blacked out. When I woke . . . the bandits were carrying me . . . but I was . . . ?'

He made a waving motion with his hands around his head.

'Hallucinating,' said Katya.

His brow furrowed. He shrugged. 'They took me to river, then . . . waterfall, yes?'

'You went over a waterfall?'

'No . . . under . . . we climbed . . .' Again he signalled with his hands. Flowing water with one, and then going beneath it with the other. 'Caves . . . they took us to caves . . .'

Dr Leota was nodding. 'The mountains are riddled with them. There is so much water flowing down, they erode the limestone, which makes caves and tunnels that go on for miles. Perfect place to hide.'

'I was sick,' said Joe, 'fever, could not walk. Big cave. My bandits . . . joined other bandits . . . they have . . . prisoner. Dr Roper. She treat my burns, give me medicine, but she did not have enough. But she got me well enough to escape. She helped me. Without her, I would be dead.'

'She was well?' Katya asked.

'I think she had fever too. She was scared. The bandits, some wanted to kill her. Others wanted to ask for money.'

'Ransom,' said Father Damian. 'It happens all the time. You see, they have no loyalty. They get hired to kill someone, but then they think they can make extra money asking for ransom, and then they kill you anyway. They are not to be trusted.'

'How long ago was this?' Michael asked.

'I was two nights in the forest after I escaped.'

'And two nights here in the hospital,' said Dr Leota.

'So she could still be alive?'

'With God's will,' said Father Damian.

Joe was given a bed in the dorm, and soon fell into an exhausted sleep – although not until he had sat with Katya, Michael and Dr Leota over her laptop, studying Google maps and NASA satellite images, trying to pinpoint exactly where the caves might be.

When Joe was finally sent to bed, Michael joined them in studying the images on the screen. 'Isn't that . . . ?'

'Mount Taron. Joe reckons he was carried across the foothills, along *here*, and then into the river and upstream *here* – but it's a huge area and there could be dozens of waterfalls.'

'Do you think he could find his way back?'

'He thinks he can.'

Dr Leota was shaking his head. 'Joe is a bright boy, and I don't think he would lie to us, but he has been very seriously ill, he's suffered hallucinations and memory loss. Now he *says* the memory has returned, but we just can't be sure. He might have jumbled what he's heard here over the past few days into what he thinks are memories.'

Father Damian was also doubtful. 'You don't know these people like I do. They will tell you what they want to hear if there's food or shelter or money in it. He might even be working for the bandits. They may be thinking of the ransom they could ask for if they could lure Dr Kincaid into their trap, rather than some obscure scientist who happens to be related to him.'

'No,' said Katya, 'Joe wouldn't do that.'

Michael drummed his fingers on the table. 'I like Joe,' he said, 'but we don't know anything about him for sure. It *could* all just be bull.'

'OK,' said Katya. 'Maybe it's time to speak to the boss.'

She stood up, lifted her mobile phone and stepped outside. Father Damian strode off to the kitchen to hunt for more food. Michael and Dr Leota studied the local maps some more until Katya reappeared. She looked considerably glummer than before she went out.

'Well?'

She took her seat and folded her hands before her on the table. 'Not good,' she said. She blew air out of her cheeks. 'Dr Kincaid has found his sister's camp. Destroyed. And some of her clothes, covered in blood. The bandits have definitely taken her, but he doesn't know if she's even alive.'

'Then all the more reason for us to find this cave.'

'No. For one thing they've been tracking the bandits, and they're going in the opposite direction to where Joe is saying they are. And for another, he's been talking to our experts at HQ. They've been able to call in a favour with the US military and redirect a military spy drone to take a closer look at Mount Taron, and it looks like there is some volcanic activity.'

'How serious?'

'Serious enough that Bailey has the inflatable back

in the water already and has bypassed us on the way back to Put Put. He's going to take the chopper up for an even closer look.'

'They're abandoning us!'

'No. They're just getting their priorities right, Michael.'

'Leaving us to twiddle our thumbs.'

'They'll come and get us as soon as they're done.'

'What about Joe, what about the caves?'

'I told Dr Kincaid, that's all I could do. He was upset about finding all the blood. He wasn't in the mood for a discussion.'

Michael stood up. 'Great. So I might as well go back to bed then.'

'Michael . . .'

He walked out.

Katya shook her head after him. She understood why he was angry, and she felt a little bit like that herself; but she also knew Dr Kincaid was right. They *were* part of SOS, but very small and junior parts. They just couldn't expect always to be at the heart of everything that was going on. Joe's information wasn't definite enough to divert precious resources to investigate it.

Father Damian wasn't the least concerned by news

of the volcano. 'It'll smoke for a while and then go back to sleep,' he said. 'Which is exactly what I'm going to do.'

He gave Katya a theatrical wink and returned to his bed. He still had a leg of chicken in one of his large hands.

When she was sure he was gone, Katya also left. She stood outside. Dawn was about an hour away yet. She sniffed, wondering if there would be any hint of smoke or fire in the air, but there was nothing beyond the slightly musty smell of the surrounding forest.

There was movement behind and she turned to find Dr Leota.

'This is my home,' he said, 'so I hope Father Damian is right.'

'So do I. But . . .' Katya trailed off.

Dr Leota sighed. 'Yes. In medicine we ignore symptoms at our peril.'

'What . . . what are you saying?'

Dr Leota was staring into the night, but his chin was slightly elevated, as if he was looking up.

'*If*, and it's a huge if, if Mount Taron is going to erupt, and Dr Roper really is in there, then waiting for Dr Kincaid to finish his search somewhere else is going to waste an awful lot of time. Sometimes you just have to follow your instincts.'

He raised an eyebrow, then turned away without another word.

Katya stared after him. Did he . . . ? Was he suggesting . . . ? Good God . . . he *was* suggesting. Katya smiled suddenly. Dr Leota was absolutely right. If there was even a tiny chance that Dr Roper was alive in the caves, then they had a duty to find out. If they didn't have the approval or support of their comrades, then that was how it would have to be. It had worked for them in the Arctic; it could just as well work for them now.

Katya charged for the dorm, yelling Michael's name.

Chapter Fifteen

The last words they heard from Father Damian as they slipped away from the river bank were: 'I am forbidding you to go! I have a responsibility to look after you!'

There was absolutely nothing he could do about it. They were on a mission. They were determined. They were excited. They were scared. The adrenaline was pumping. They'd hired the same small, low-lying craft that had brought Joe back to St Mark's, but left its pilot at the mission station. They had packed in the supplies the Artists had been forced to leave behind when the third inflatable was badly damaged. They had one handgun, one knife and a night-vision pocketscope. Katya was at the back, steering, Michael in the middle and Joe at the front, shouting directions when needed – and they *were* needed. Before very long the river split into a bewildering series of tributaries, branches and streams that would have flummoxed a seasoned explorer with a detailed map. Joe, who did not even come from this part of the island, and who had been delirious by the time he stumbled into St Mark's, was suddenly very certain of which route to take, and all they could do was trust him.

The sun, prevented from penetrating the trees by the height and thickness of the forest canopy, seemed to be focusing more intently on the exposed stretch of river. They could have kept to the greater shade at the banks, but preferred the heat to the surprises that came with skirting the edges – the waterfalls flashing out of nowhere, the magnetic suction of their whirlpools, the falling branches, overhanging snakes and the occasional flurry of birds as a crocodile slipped into the water.

'This way! This way!' Joe indicated excitedly as Katya steered the craft.

They sweated and they burned, but they motored on relentlessly all morning until, eventually, the river narrowed, the current strengthening with the incline as they rose up into the mountains; it all became too powerful for their little craft. It was built for hauling goods along largely passive waterways, not battling torrents and butting off jagged rocks. They could go no further.

They beached the boat and hid it in the shallow undergrowth, marked its position on Katya's GPS, shouldered their rucksacks and began their journey anew, this time through the trees, but always keeping the river bank in sight. Their muscles ached. Insects *attacked*. It didn't seem to affect Joe, leading the way, in the slightest, but behind him Katya spent half her time slapping at her face; it was the only part of her skin that was exposed. Michael had tried wearing a long-sleeved shirt, but the sopping heat was too much. He had stripped it off and was now just in a T-shirt; bites peppered his arms.

They rested for ten minutes at a curve in the river. Michael and Katya drank bottles of water. Joe just plunged his head into the river and drank. Then he jumped in and repeatedly dived under. Michael knew there were numerous fish in there with teeth that could take off your leg or inject poison into your blood. Joe didn't seem to care.

Michael shook his head. 'He either knows something we don't,' he said to Katya, 'or he's mad.'

Katya, perched securely on a rock, took another drink and smiled. 'Well, he seems to be doing fine.

If you worried about every risk there is out here, you'd probably never leave home.'

Michael shook his head doubtfully. 'Mad,' he said. 'It's not even the fish, it's drinking the water.'

'Maybe you get used to it.'

'Doubt it.'

Joe pulled himself out of the river and on to the rock beside Katya. A moment later a crocodile almost four metres long eased past, two eyes scoping them out before coasting away to the opposite bank.

All three of them stared at it.

And then they got up and started walking without saying a word, at least for the first hundred metres. Then suddenly Joe began laughing, and then Katya, and finally Michael joined in – it was a mixture of relief and barely restrained hysteria. They continued to climb, only now it was to the accompaniment of slightly crazed outbursts of giggling.

Joe forged ahead. He was not long out of a coma, but his natural athleticism put both Katya, and particularly Michael, to shame.

Just ahead, Katya tripped over a slippery root and hit the ground hard. Michael caught up, and reached down to help her up.

She ignored his hand. 'I'm fine,' she said.

He crouched down beside her and looked at her scraped and bloody knee. 'So I see.'

He pulled off his rucksack and began to search for his medikit.

'I'm quite capable of—' Katya began.

'Oh, be quiet,' said Michael. He found the kit, snapped it open, and began to clean the wound. As he did he looked up to where Joe was already a hundred metres ahead. 'Hold on!' he shouted.

Joe waved back, and rested against an outcrop of rock.

Katya said, quietly, 'He's so certain of where he's going.'

'He's certainly focused. Could be some kind of a trap, lure us into the middle of nowhere and rob us.'

'Why would he do that?'

'Maybe driven mad by seeing his father murdered, his village burned.'

'It's just made him more determined to get back at the bandits. It's revenge that's driving him on.'

'Could be. But he hasn't even looked at a map. It's like he has an internal GPS.'

'Michael, people were finding their way around long before there was GPS. And if there's any chance of saving Dr Roper, then we have to try, don't we?'

Michael nodded. He finished patching Katya up. It wasn't a bad cut, but out here, it was best to be safe. He gave her a hand up.

'Thanks,' she said.

'No problem,' said Michael. 'Just remember, it's good to have a back-up plan. So if we get ambushed, you fight them off, I'll go for help.'

She smiled. 'Just like you to run away.'

'Don't worry, I'd come back. Eventually.'

He winked.

They marched on.

It was just beginning to get dark when Joe stopped about twenty metres ahead of them. To their left the river had widened again. It was flowing faster, all churned up and muddy. As they caught up they saw what had stopped him: a waterfall, high and thundering out of the mountain about three hundred metres away.

'Is that it?' Michael asked.

Joe nodded.

Michael turned to Katya. 'How are we ever going to . . . ?'

But she held up a finger to hush him. She raised the night scope. 'There's a guard,' she said.

'Plan?' asked Michael.

'We rest up until it's completely dark, we go in.'

'How do we get past the guard?'

'Stealth.'

'Simple as that?'

'Simple as that.'

They backed up around the curve until they were sure they couldn't be observed. Katya took a tent from her rucksack and snapped it quickly and easily into position. They climbed inside. It was as much for protection from the insects as anything. Michael and Katya ate power bars.

Joe nibbled suspiciously at his. He said, 'It is like eating . . . wood,' and gave it back to Katya. He wordlessly slipped out of the tent and zipped it closed behind him.

Michael and Katya looked at each other in the gloom.

In the rainforest, it was never quiet. It was probably more *alive* than any remote place on earth. But they couldn't hear Joe.

'What is he doing?' Michael asked.

'He's probably just . . . I don't know.'

'Having a pee,' said Michael.

'Yeah. Possibly.'

They kept their eyes on the tent zip. It would soon be pitch black. They had followed a boy who had very recently been suffering from hallucinations into the middle of nowhere.

'Or . . .'

'Don't think about it. You're just being paranoid.'

Michael nodded.

Katya pulled her rucksack closer and opened one of the side pockets. She produced the Browning Hi-Power 9mm handgun and checked the action.

'Now who's being paranoid?'

'Even paranoids are right sometimes.'

Michael delved into his own rucksack and produced the hunting knife. He removed it from its sheath.

He said, 'Do you have a problem with shooting someone?'

'Nope.'

'Do you shout a warning first?'

Katya tossed him the flashlight. 'When it comes to it, you illuminate the target, blind him. I'll do the rest.'

Ten minutes went by.

Then: movement outside.

Katya raised the gun and centred it on the zip.

Michael gripped the knife in his right hand. If Joe had led bandits back to camp, the knife would be useless. So, probably, would Katya's gun. He had the flashlight in his left hand. He pointed it at the flap, but with the power off.

'Joe, is that you?' Michael called softly.

No response.

The zip moved slowly down. Sweat rolled across Katya's brow at exactly the same pace.

Michael swallowed.

Katya's finger was already curled around the trigger and very subtly squeezing.

The flap opened.

Michael flicked on the flashlight.

Katya squeezed the trigger.

But stopped, just as Joe's smiling face was illuminated.

He threw something in.

Something moving.

Michael threw himself backwards.

And Katya started laughing. 'Mighty Michael,' she said, 'scared of a fish.'

'Bloody hell,' said Michael.

Chapter Sixteen

They cooked it on a small stove inside the tent. Joe added handfuls of *stuff* neither of them recognized in the glow of the flashlight. He said he'd picked it off the surrounding rocks.

When they'd finished eating Katya said, 'That was fantastic. Even though I'm a vegetarian, that is one of the nicest meals I have ever tasted.'

'I'm not sure you still qualify as a vegetarian,' said Michael.

'Vegetarianism is a state of mind,' said Katya, adamantly.

'No,' Michael pointed out, '*vegetable* is a state of mind. *Vegetarianism* is just . . . *nuts.*'

Katya smiled. 'I'm not getting into an argument,' she said.

'Because I'd win.'

'Because we have bigger fish to fry.'

She nodded in the direction of the waterfall and the mountain.

Michael felt a sudden rush of apprehension. Eating had been a distraction, but it was now getting very close to the time to move out.

Katya had noticed that Joe had been silent throughout the meal. 'You OK?' she asked. Joe nodded, but it wasn't very convincing. 'You don't have to go with us. You've brought us to the caves, that's more than enough.'

'No. Dr Roper saved me, I must also save her.'

'Then what is it?' Michael asked.

Joe glanced back outside, towards the river. His brow furrowed in confusion. 'When I go in. The water is hot.'

'Well, it's certainly warmer than at home,' said Michael, 'and as for the Arctic—'

'No . . . look.'

Joe indicated his bare legs. Michael angled the flashlight down, and saw to his surprise and shock that they were both red and blistering right up to his knees.

'Oh my God,' said Katya, immediately crawling over to him. 'Why didn't you say?'

Joe shrugged. 'It does not hurt much. But the water?

The fish was floating on top. They are dead. All dead.'

'And you let us *eat* it?' Michael asked, without really thinking.

Katya glared at him. 'Give me the medikit, Michael. *Now.*'

He got it. Katya set to work applying a cooling balm. She said to Joe, 'I'm not going to bandage you, out here they'd get soaked and infected as soon as we start walking. But these need to be treated properly.' Katya looked up at Michael. 'We should really get him back to base.'

Michael nodded, but his eyes said *no*. 'A couple of hours won't make much difference.'

'You don't know that. Burns, the sooner you treat them the better.'

'We can't turn back now.'

'And I'm not going back,' said Joe.

Michael punched him lightly on the shoulder. 'Good man,' he said.

'OK,' said Katya. 'Then we need to get moving.'

Michael nodded beside her. 'If the water running through the caves is boiling, the bandits aren't going to stay in there for long.'

'The water could be boiling up in some places, not in others,' said Katya. 'There'll be a lot of sources converging on the river. Maybe Joe just got unlucky, stepped into a hot spot. But you're right. If they decide to move out, there are probably multiple exits. There's a good chance we'll lose them, and that means losing Dr Roper as well. So let's get there asap.'

But before they could move, the ground itself moved beneath them. Subtle. But definite.

'Feel that?' asked Michael.

'Felt it,' said Katya.

They moved through the darkness, careful at first not to make any noise, but then quickly realizing that it didn't really matter, that the thunder of the waterfall was covering anything. They could have sung at the tops of their voices and it wouldn't have been heard.

Michael went first, carefully picking out his progress across the rocks and raising his night scope every few metres, training it on the waterfall, looking for signs of light or life through the cascading curtain hurtling out of the limestone breach in Mount Taron. Katya moved behind him, carefully treading where Michael stepped first. She had the Browning handgun in her side pocket. Every couple of minutes her hand snaked inside, tracing its outline, seeking reassurance. Joe brought up the rear. Katya glanced back at him often.

He had said his burns didn't hurt, but she was sure he was in agony. He was being brave. For them. Katya wasn't sure if she could have carried on with such injuries. She knew that all the SOS training couldn't really prepare you for pain.

They were now so close to the waterfall that they had to communicate through a very rudimentary sign language which consisted of little more than pointing upwards and nodding. They skirted around a slippery outcrop which brought them level with the waterfall and soaked them in hot spray. Until they were right up beside it, it had continued to look like a solid, impenetrable curtain. But then, just as a curtain can billow out in the slightest breeze, leaving a vacuum behind, they glimpsed the gap they needed and went for it. That was probably the scariest moment, like stepping through an open door without knowing what lay behind, an ordinary room or a house of horror.

Before they took that step Michael indicated to Katya that he wanted the gun. She hesitated before handing it over. Michael grasped it, nodded at her, then stepped into the gap, gun out before him in his left hand, and the right holding the night scope up to his eye. He disappeared into the misty spray and utter darkness, leaving Katya and Joe alone and terrified on the outside.

A full minute passed.

Then Michael stepped out of the curtain, with one finger already raised to his lips for silence, before indicating for them to follow him. He took Katya's hand and placed it on his shoulder, and Joe put his hand on Katya's. Michael stepped back into the darkness and Katya and Joe followed.

Two differences were immediately apparent. Katya had thought it dark *outside* – but this was of a different magnitude. Utter and complete blackness. Then there was the sound: once they entered the mouth of the cave the thunder of the waterfall quietened to a quite astonishing extent, as if someone had just turned the volume down. Michael pressed the night scope into Katya's hand and whispered, 'Thirty metres, to your left.'

She raised it. Scanned. It took her a moment to realize what she was looking at. Then she caught her breath as she saw one of the bandits, half hidden behind a rock, with a rifle leaning on it and pointing directly at her. She immediately lowered the night scope, as if that might somehow miraculously protect her, but fully expecting any moment to be cut down by a high-powered bullet. But nothing happened, and then she felt Michael's mouth at her ear and heard his urgent whisper, 'He's fast asleep.'

Katya raised the night scope – and sure enough, the bandit had propped himself behind the rock, and settled the rifle in a perfect firing position to cover the mouth of the cave. And then he had nodded off.

She turned the scope back on Michael, and he signalled for them to move forward.

They eased past the guard, their hearts in their mouths, and pressed onwards. Besides the night scope, Michael walked with his flashlight switched on, but covering the beam with his hand, thus allowing only the faintest glow to escape. It was just enough for them to pick their way up the incline. The river rushed past to their left, and sat flush against the opposite bank, meaning that the path they were taking was the only way ahead. If someone came towards them, or followed up behind, they would be trapped. It should have become cooler the deeper they moved into the cave system, but the air remained warm, and grew warmer. The mountain continued to rumble and vibrate, but again it was subtle, enough to worry them, but not enough to finally scare them off.

After ten minutes of energy-sapping upward

progress the path began to level out. The cave ceiling, which had been only a few metres above their heads, grew higher with each step they took. The path widened out, until eventually they were walking on an undulating plane within a huge chamber cut in two by the river. Stalagmites peppered the floor; doubtless their opposites pricked down from the distant ceiling. Ahead of them: the glow of fire.

Michael killed the flashlight. They crouched down among the stalags. Michael raised the night scope, focused in on the fire for thirty seconds, before handing it to Katya.

'What do you think?' he whispered.

She took her time, making sure. 'Twelve bandits. Most sleeping, but there's two by the fire, talking. '

'I don't see Dr Roper.'

'I know. But there's a second fire?'

Michael had missed it completely. He took the scope back and she directed him to the right. There was the black mass of a boulder, and a meagre glow coming from behind it.

'Good one. But we're not going to find out from here. Do you think we could go wide across *there*, and come in behind them?'

Katya handed the scope to Joe and indicated their

planned approach. Joe studied it before putting the scope back in her hand and nodding.

'OK,' said Katya. She fingered the handgun once more.

They moved off. The main fire was perhaps a hundred metres away. With the river wider in this chamber and its banks higher, its sound was oddly diminished; conversely their own steps on the limestone floor seemed to reverberate. It wasn't as loud as they thought, but it enhanced their nervousness and slowed them down. They knew that if they were caught in the open they'd have nowhere to hide.

It took them five minutes to reach the far side of the cavern, and then they began to make their way back towards the second fire, which was now no longer shielded by the rock but glowing bright. When Michael judged they were sufficiently close he crouched down among the stalags, with Katya and Joe on either side of him. He wiped at his brow, which was thick with sweat. He pulled at his shirt, which was uncomfortably stuck to his back. He raised the night scope, his heart beating wildly. If Dr Roper was here, then it justified their journey. If it was just a bandit hideout then they'd put themselves in danger on the word of a hallucinating teenager. He took a deep breath, then let it out slowly. He raised the scope and focused in.

'Well?' Katya whispered.

'Give me a minute . . .'

'Well?'

Michael remained infuriatingly quiet while he studied the scene. Then he lowered the night scope.

'*Well?*'

'It's her.'

Katya's heart soared – though not so much that she absolutely believed him. 'Lemme see . . .' she gushed and grabbed for the scope. Caught off guard Michael automatically pulled it away, but their hands collided and he lost his grip on it.

It fell.

But barely a centimetre from it clattering noisily to the ground, Joe's hand shot out and caught it.

'Sorry . . . sorry . . .' Katya whispered. 'Sorry . . .'

Joe managed a half smile and held it out to her.

Chastened, she shook her head. 'You first.'

Joe raised it while Katya tried to steady her thundering heart. After thirty seconds he held it out to her and she took it *very* carefully.

Katya trained the scope on the fire, which was perhaps fifty metres distant. Yes, indeed, she was pretty certain it was Dr Roper, lying on a single blanket which was partially wrapped around her, but facing the fire so that her face was illuminated.

'She's not alone,' said Katya. 'There's another woman, other side of the fire.'

Michael nodded. 'Guarding her?'

'Not doing a very good job. Looks like she's sleeping.' Katya lowered the scope.

'So, do we have a plan?' Michael asked.

'Hasn't changed. Sneak in, sneak out.'

'What if the other woman wakes up?'

'We make sure she sees the gun.'

'What if we get rumbled by someone else?'

'We start shooting.'

'*We?*'

'Well, you can make threatening gestures with your hunting knife.'

Michael smiled. Katya smiled.

'Long way from boarding school now, aren't you, Michael?'

'You could say that.'

'Wish you were back there?'

'Not in a million years.'

'OK then. Let's do this.'

Michael eyed the scope once more, this time

concentrating on the bandits' fire on the other side of the rock. The two men who had been talking now appeared to be asleep. Michael stepped forward. Katya and Joe rose and began to follow. If it came to a fight, Katya didn't want to waste any time fumbling for the gun, so she slipped her hand into her pocket to pull it out.

Except it wasn't there.

'*Wait!*' she hissed.

Michael stopped and looked back.

Katya crouched back down and felt blindly around her, but couldn't locate the gun. She was confused. If it had fallen out it would definitely have made a very loud noise.

'What are you doing?' Michael demanded impatiently.

'The gun, I can't find it.'

'*Here . . .*'

Michael produced the torch, switched it on, but was careful to cover most of the beam. He knelt beside her and studied the surrounding rocks.

'I don't know how I could have dropped it.'

Michael widened the circumference of the beam, allowing it to crawl across the surface until it reached Joe's feet.

'Joe . . . do you think you could help?' Michael began.

Joe didn't move. Michael angled the beam upwards until it settled on their friend's torso and head.

Joe had the gun in his hand.

And he was pointing it at Michael.

'Joe . . . ?'

'Sorry,' said Joe. He raised the gun above his head and pulled the trigger. The bullet exploded with a deafening roar.

And before its echo had even begun to disappear Joe was shouting, 'Over here! They are here!'

Chapter Seventeen

They had been tracking the bandits for eight sweaty hours before Mr Crown called a halt. They needed to rest up properly, take on liquids and eat. Technically, Dr Kincaid was in charge, and could have insisted on drinking and grazing on the hoof. They were closing in on his sister, and they couldn't afford to lose any time. But the truth was that he could hardly manage another step. He was exhausted. The adrenaline of the pursuit could only carry him so far. Out here in the rainforest, Mr Crown was the expert. He knew how far a body could be pushed.

So they stopped, and broke out a stove, and bottles of water.

'Sit.'

Dr Kincaid looked up – everyone looked *up* when Mr Crown was involved, he was that tall and imposing

– to find the Artists' real action man looming over him.

'Sorry? What?'

'We've been stopped for five minutes, and you still haven't sat down. The trackers can get their own food and water. They're younger and fitter than you. This is designed for *you* to get a rest, replenish energy. So sit.'

Dr Kincaid sat.

Mr Crown handed him a bottle of water. 'Drink.'

He drank. He wiped a hand across his brow. 'We're getting close,' he said. 'I'm sure of it.'

Mr Crown didn't look convinced.

Dr Kincaid was an optimist. It was the only way he could cope with all the depressing things he had to deal with on an almost daily basis. Mr Crown on the other hand was . . . well, if not a pessimist exactly, then perhaps a pragmatist. Always looking at things realistically, soberly and never getting too excited or too negative. But what *wasn't* there to be excited about? thought Dr Kincaid. Hadn't the trackers identified the very Nike training shoes his sister had been wearing, and hadn't they been following their distinctive pattern all day? And wasn't his sister helping them even further by dropping little pieces of evidence along the way? He had in his pocket three different items the trackers had spotted dropped on the trail and excitedly pounced upon: the Twix wrapper, one of a pair of earrings he had given her for Christmas five years before, and then, five kilometres later, the second one.

'Tracker Mark thinks we're only thirty minutes behind them, the tracks are that fresh.'

'*If* we are,' Mr Crown replied, his voice low, calm, 'then we have to be careful. We don't want to walk into a trap. *You* would make a much more important and valuable hostage than your sister. Or if we stumble into them unannounced there might be a shooting match, and that's exactly what we don't want. We pinpoint their position and then we call in support, surround them and negotiate from a position of strength. Most importantly, we show patience.'

'Patience. Absolutely.'

'Eat,' said Mr Crown, and handed Dr Kincaid a power bar.

He took it. He unwrapped it. He took a first bite. Mr Crown nodded and walked off to consult with Tracker Mark. Dr Kincaid stuffed the power bar into one pocket and produced his satellite phone from the other. He called Bonsoir and immediately flinched at the cacophony of sound that went with the flight of a helicopter. The logistics expert shouted that they were just approaching Mount Taron.

'*Now?* But you left ages ago!'

'Yup! We ran into a little local trouble.'

'You both OK?'

'I'm fine, but I'm not so sure about Bailey.'

'What's wrong with him?'

'He seems intent on flying far too close to this damn volcano, that's what's wrong with him.'

'OK, well, that's no surprise. Tell me what happened, and then tell me about the mountain.'

'Someone shot up the chopper a bit while we were gone. Apparently some people *really* don't like us.'

'Much damage?'

'Nope, but took us a while to check and make some minor repairs. My friend at the controls here was furious. Was like they'd shot one of his children. But it doesn't seem to stop him putting his children near a *great big fire.*'

'Is that what you're seeing?'

'Well, it's kind of hard to tell. There's an awful lot of smoke. But they say there's no smoke without fire. Indonesian air traffic control has established a no-fly zone, which Bailey seems to be completely ignoring.'

'Tell him one thing, he'll invariably do the other.'

'I'm just uploading data now to HQ. We'll know pretty soon if this baby's gonna blow, or she's just letting off steam.'

'Excellent. Tell Bailey not to get too close.'

'Bailey – the boss says not to get too close.'

'What's that?' Dr Kincaid heard Bailey respond. 'You want to get closer? Going in!'

Dr Kincaid smiled. Bailey was the best pilot he'd ever met. He had to be in order to take the kind of risks he took.

Dr Kincaid briefly updated Bonsoir on the progress of their search for Dr Roper, then just before cutting the line asked if Michael and Katya were proving helpful.

There was a brief hesitation, and then, 'Uhm, that would be a no.'

'They messing you around?'

'They probably would be, if they were here.'

Dr Kincaid sighed. 'Tell me.'

'Well. We landed at the mission to pick them up. Except they'd taken off on their own little mission.'

'Mission? What on earth . . . ?'

'They had some local information that your sister was being held upriver.'

'My sister . . . ? Upriver? But upriver would be . . .'

'Yep, in the general direction of that seething ball of magma beneath us.'

'Great. I want them out of there. You're tracking them?'

'Yes. Of course.'

'So you know exactly where they are?'

'Ahm. Yes. Kind of.'

Dr Kincaid could hardly believe what he was hearing. He was worried enough about his sister. He didn't need this. He *definitely* didn't need this.

'Spit it out.'

'Well, the tracking devices in their equipment and clothes have taken them as far as the lower reaches of Mount Taron.'

'And?'

'Well, then we lost them.'

'What do you mean you lost them? Those devices are indestructible.'

'Well, I wouldn't go that far. In that huge amounts of lava could probably do a pretty good job on them.'

'You're saying . . .'

'No, most likely explanation is that the volcano is interfering with the signal.'

There was a long, uncomfortable radio silence.

Then Dr Kincaid said with quiet but complete

authority, 'I want you to stop what you're doing. Go and find them.'

'I'm sorry, we can't go that low. The air down there is thick with ash, it would clog up the engine in a couple of minutes.'

'I don't care *how* you do it!' Dr Kincaid exploded. 'I just want them the hell out of there!'

Dr Leota was in the hospital, tending to one of the patients who could not be evacuated, when a child came hobbling in. The boy, nine years old, had been treated for a badly broken leg six months previously and had never left St Mark's; he survived by running errands and sweeping up in exchange for food. The doctor was surprised to see him: he had ordered him into one of the boats taking his patients and staff downriver in advance of the predicted eruption of Mount Taron.

'Doctor! Doctor! It is snow!!'

Dr Leota smiled indulgently before glancing out of the open shutters. He gave a start. It did indeed look as if it was snowing – which would have been a miracle indeed for the constantly steamy rainforest. But he couldn't blame the boy for his mistake.

Dr Leota calmly finished what he was doing before

making his way outside. The very few who had not fled the mission station, and who were capable of walking, were already in the yard, looking up at the sky with considerable trepidation.

It wasn't snow. It was ash.

Even as they watched, it seemed to grow thicker, and began to coat everything. Father Damian emerged from the church and stood beside Dr Leota, his black shirt already dotted with it.

'If you haven't already started praying,' said Dr Leota, 'I'd start right now.'

Chapter Eighteen

They had been betrayed, and the reason for it became clear within minutes of them being surrounded by baying, shouting, madly gesticulating bandits, dragged forward to the fire and thrown down and screamed at. As they lay there, terrified, Dr Roper came hurtling out from behind the rock and yelled at the bandits to leave them alone, barging two of them out of the way and slapping another; a fourth raised a machete to her, but she didn't back down. They spoke angrily among themselves, and then barked orders at her to move Michael and Katya across to her own fire, promising that she would be brutally punished if they tried to escape. Michael and Katya raised themselves cautiously – and almost the first thing they saw was Joe, not standing triumphant at having suckered them into the bandits' camp, but looking miserable while being urgently kissed by the woman who had been lying beside Dr Roper.

Joe looked directly at them. 'I am sorry. They said they would kill my mother if I did not bring you here.'

Michael nodded sullenly. Katya tried to say something to Joe, but couldn't find the right words. She just kind of shrugged as Dr Roper ushered them over to her fire.

They sat awkwardly, still frightened, still angry. Joe's mother was holding on to him so tightly she didn't look as if she would ever let him go again.

'You shouldn't have come,' said Dr Roper, 'but I've never been so glad to see you in my life.' She dropped her voice to an urgent whisper. 'Where are the others?'

'Others?' asked Michael.

'My brother? The Artists? What's the plan? We need to make a move before the big boss arrives.' She looked from Michael to Katya.

'Well . . .' said Michael.

Dr Roper's eyes narrowed. 'You can *tell* me. I know how my brother operates, but still . . . You're like decoys, or scouts, you allowed yourself to be captured so you could report back on how many bandits there are, or what they want. Isn't that right?'

Now that Michael could see her properly, he registered the desperation in her eyes and her wan complexion. It was as if the showdown with the bandits had been her final act of defiance. Now she looked like a broken woman. He had to remember that she wasn't part of SOS, she was a scientist, a researcher, interested in animals and nature. She had been violently seized by these bandits, marched through the rainforest and then held hostage for days underneath a massive volcano, all the time in fear for her life.

'That's right,' said Katya. Michael turned to her, surprised. 'And he sends his love and promises he will get you out of here, but for now, you just have to do what we say. That's the way he wants to play it.'

Dr Roper rubbed the palm of her hand into her smoke-reddened eyes.

'Yes . . . yes, of course . . . I understand . . . Best not to know in case they . . . force it out of me. Sending children, that's clever, that's clever . . .'

She seemed to fold in on herself, collapsing down where she sat, in front of the fire, and burying her head in her hands. She began to sob, and her shoulders began to shake.

'I'm sorry, I'm sorry . . .' she cried. 'It's just . . .'

'It's OK,' said Katya, putting an arm around her. 'It's OK.'

Katya's eyes met Michael's. It was very clear to both of them that it was *very far* from OK.

Four bandits sat in a semi-circle just on the edge of the firelight; every twenty minutes another arrived to make sure his comrades hadn't fallen asleep. If either Michael or Katya moved, they were growled at. Katya asked for water. She was ignored.

'Not looking good,' said Michael.

'Uhm. No.'

The bandits had seized their rucksacks and torn them apart. Now their clothes and equipment littered the cave. They had been particularly excited to find Katya's laptop, but had then frisbeed it across the floor when they discovered they couldn't get an internet signal. Michael's hunting knife was now the prized possession of a young bandit sporting a wispy moustache and wearing a too-tight *Reebok* T-shirt. Another with frizzy hair and a Manchester United football top had the Browning handgun stuck in his waistband. Nobody seemed to be in charge.

After what felt like an eternity – and they'd been stripped of their watches, so they really had no idea how long it actually was – Joe approached carrying two plastic plates loosely scattered with rice, and several small pieces of fatty meat which they didn't recognize and didn't even attempt to eat. He set the food down wordlessly. But he didn't go. He hovered.

Katya said, 'Sit down, Joe, it's OK.'

He stayed where he was. He looked at Michael – who was aware of his scrutiny, but ignored him, instead choosing to gaze intently into the fire.

'Michael?' said Katya. 'He had no choice.'

'Uh-huh.'

'You would do the same for your own mother.'

Katya made it her business to know everything about everything, so he knew she was aware that his mother was dead. But he didn't know if she meant it cruelly, or was just trying to make a point. Would he really betray two friends so callously? Michael looked up at Joe. He gave a slight nod of his head. It was the best Joe was going to get. Katya reached up and took his hand and pulled him down gently.

'How are the burns, Joe?'

Joe looked pointedly at Michael and said, 'They promised they would let my mother live if I brought you back. Not me. They will kill me. But I could not let them kill my mother.'

Michael looked up. 'So are they letting her go?'

Joe shook his head.

'Guess we've all been suckered,' said Michael.

They weren't the only ones.

Many kilometres to the west, Tracker Mark stopped suddenly and dropped into a crouch, with one hand raised to warn Dr Kincaid, Mr Crown and the other members of their small pursuing band. Mr Crown immediately slipped his automatic rifle from over his shoulder and raised it into a firing position. He scanned the track ahead: it had widened into a small patch of land which at one time had been cleared and a primitive stone house erected. The building had long since fallen into disrepair and the garden surrounding it was overgrown, but someone had removed a broken table from inside and propped it up in the long grass. At the foot of the table there was a pair of trainers. On the table top there sat a mobile phone.

It began to ring.

Mr Crown's finger tightened on the trigger. He raised himself and moved forward.

'It's a trap!' Dr Kincaid hissed.

Mr Crown shook his head. 'They want to talk. A phone ringing out here would travel for miles, so if this is the first time it has rung it means they knew we were about to arrive here. We're being watched. Answer the phone.'

As Mr Crown moved his rifle slowly around the clearing Dr Kincaid hurried forward. He reached the table and looked down at his sister's Nike trainers. He realized with a sickening lurch that they hadn't been following her at all; they'd been following her shoes. One of the bandits had been wearing them to deliberately throw them off the trail.

Dr Kincaid picked up the phone.

'Kincaid.' His voice was calm, strong, confident.

'Dr Kincaid. How pleasant to talk to you again. I hope you have enjoyed a pleasant walk.'

He recognized the strongly accented voice in an instant. He met hundreds of new people every week of his life, and it was one of his great talents that he had an excellent memory for names and faces and voices. He knew immediately that this was the man in the dirty white suit they had encountered at the Put Put Mission Station.

'Say what you have to say,' said Dr Kincaid.

'Very well. There has been a change of circumstances, Dr Kincaid. I no longer require one million US dollars for the return of your sister.'

Dr Kincaid's eyes narrowed. He knew that whatever was coming was unlikely to be good news.

'You see, I not only have her, I also have your children. For the return of all three, the price is now five million US dollars, and I require it by tomorrow or I will kill them. You chose to interfere in my island, Dr Kincaid, and so you must pay. And to let you know how serious I am . . .'

A single shot rang out.

Tracker Mark fell.

He was dead before he hit the ground.

Chapter Nineteen

The continuous rumblings beneath, above and around and the growing heat made it impossible for anyone to sleep. Dr Roper lay with her eyes open, staring into the dark. The bandits yelled at each other. Michael and Katya whispered plan and counter-plan, argued, made up and argued again. No matter which way they looked at it they were prisoners of a gang of murderous bandits, trapped inside a volcano that looked likely to erupt at any time, and they had no means of escape that did not seem likely to end with them either being shot down or hacked to death with machetes. And even if by some miracle they did manage to outrun their pursuers they could not also hope to bring Dr Roper along with them at a similar pace. That was, after all, the purpose of their mission.

So they waited, and sweated. The shouting of the

bandits grew louder, and several fights broke out, with much pointing and gesticulating – a great deal of it in their direction. Michael didn't really want to know why they were fighting, because he was pretty sure it wasn't about how best to set them free. Katya thought it better to know the facts, no matter how depressing.

'They are frightened,' said Joe. 'Frightened of the heat and the moving of the earth.'

'So why don't they take us out of here?' Katya asked.

'Because they are also frightened of their boss. He told them to bring us here and wait until he arrived. He is a very bad man. When he comes, he will kill me. When he has his ransom for Dr Roper, he will kill her. When he has his money for you, he will kill you too. There is no benefit to him in letting you live. But he will at least keep you alive until the money is handed over. I will not be so lucky.'

Joe looked resigned to his fate.

Katya shook her head. 'This is madness. Unless we do something, we're all going to die, either at their hands or under a million kilos of red-hot lava. We have to do *something*.'

'Like what?' asked Michael. 'Whichever way you look at it we're stuck. As soon as we make a move they're going to be on us. We can't go *that* way, or *that* way, and the river cuts us off on that side.'

Katya's eyes widened. The *river*. It was so obvious. It was the only way of getting around the problem of hurrying Dr Roper along.

Michael saw where she was looking. 'Ah,' he said.

'We run, we jump before they can get us in their sights, the current is fast and it's only going in one direction – out of here.'

'There's a fair chance we'll get shot before we get there, and if we get there, there's a fair chance we'll drown, or pass through a hot spot and get scalded, and the guard at the entrance could spot us and we'd be sitting ducks, almost literally.'

'All true,' Katya agreed.

'And that's not to mention the fact that if we get flushed along to the mouth of the cave the current will wash us out into the waterfall and that's a forty-metre drop. And if by some miracle that doesn't kill us we still have to get out of the river and make our way back to the boat which, incidentally, is not big enough to carry all of us. Because knowing you I presume you're not just talking about Dr Roper, but Joe and his mum as well.'

'We can't leave them. We're SOS.' Katya was firm.

It was a simple statement, but it meant *everything* to

Michael. He had been an orphan. He had been abandoned. He had been ferried from one boarding school to another all of his life. He had never had a family, never had close friends or anyone to turn to. He had survived, he had become physically strong, but he was scarred, and in his more thoughtful moments – that is, when he wasn't putting his foot in something or getting into a fight – he was quite aware of it. But SOS, even though he had only been part of it for a few days, was already giving him something that he had never had in his life before: a family of his own.

And self-respect.

He gave the slightest nod.

Katya gave it back.

'OK,' she said, 'game on.'

It was not the most complicated plan in the world. Make a break for the river and jump in. Make sure Dr Roper doesn't sink. Be flushed out of a cave. If still alive: run!

Joe was all for it. He told his mother. They discussed it in animated whispers. She didn't look happy.

'Problem?' Katya asked.

'She cannot swim.'

'There won't be any time for swimming,' said Katya.

'All she has to do is float. Everyone can float.'

'Tell her,' said Michael, 'that we are going to be like poo being flushed down a toilet.'

'*Michael*,' groaned Katya.

Joe said, 'Our toilets do not flush.'

'Then think of something else. We're going, with or without her. We haven't time to mess around.'

Joe's eyes flashed angrily for a split second, but he turned and spoke quickly to his mother.

Dr Roper was still lying by the fire.

'Are you going with or without her as well?' Katya asked.

Michael made a face. Katya crossed to her and began to tell her the plan. Michel kept an eye on the bandits. They were more subdued now. Despite the overwhelming heat they were still gathered about their fire: there was something reassuring about it, as if it might somehow protect them. He looked towards the river. It was maybe fifteen metres away. Not far for him or Katya or Joe to sprint, but a long enough distance to shepherd the women across.

Katya came back. She didn't look very happy. 'I'm not sure she gets it,' she said urgently. 'I think she has malaria. She's certainly dehydrated and exhausted. And terrified. Best I could manage was to say there was a boat coming to pick us up and we'd need her to be ready for it.'

'And when she sees there's no boat?'

'We push her in, and we keep hold of her.'

'In trying to save her, we'll probably kill her.'

'If we don't try, this mountain or the bandits definitely will.'

Michael still wasn't completely happy with the plan. They needed something more, something that could even slightly increase the distant odds of their success. He moved up beside Joe.

'Joe, I need you to do something for us.'

'Tell me what you want me to do.'

'It's the fires. They're lighting up too much of the cave. We can deal with our own, but I need you to put out the bandits'. They've trusted you enough to bring us food. Go over to them, find a reason, ask for water, something, but find some way to put out those flames.'

'But they have flashlights.'

'Sure they do. But by the time they find them in the dark and work out what's going on, hopefully we'll be floating downstream.'

Joe thought about it very briefly before nodding. 'OK,' he said.

'It means you'll have further to run, and there's a pretty good chance you won't make it.'

'I am a dead man anyway. If this helps my mother, if it helps all of you, then that is good.'

Katya wasn't thrilled when he told her.

'He's fine with it,' said Michael, 'and he owes us.'

'He doesn't owe us anything, Michael. He got us here, didn't he?'

'And then sold us out.'

Katya fumed. But she also knew Michael was right. They wouldn't make the river if the cavern was still lit up. She shook her head at Michael, but gave Joe the thumbs-up and mouthed a silent thank you.

After that it was just a matter of timing. Both fires needed to go out at exactly the same time or the whole escape attempt would be pointless.

Joe gave his mother a final hug, then nodded at Michael and began to move towards the bandits' fire. Those who had been specifically tasked with keeping an eye on the hostages barked something as he moved through them, and Joe barked something back. He kept moving. They didn't attempt to stop him.

Katya moved beside Dr Roper and whispered in her ear that it was time to go. She helped her to her feet. One of the bandits snapped something at them. Joe's mother unexpectedly responded, and there was a brief exchange before she nodded at Katya. When she spoke her English was slow and broken. 'It is . . . OK . . . toilet?'

Excellent. Katya was taking the sick doctor to the toilet. That would allow her to get much closer to the river before the fire was kicked out.

'I . . . help . . . ?'

Katya nodded. Joe's mother spoke rapidly to the guard and he shrugged. All three of them began to move away from the fire.

Michael knelt and pretended to tie his lace. He scooped up one of the T-shirts their captors had thrown out of his rucksack and moved with it closer to the fire. Joe was now beside the other one. The bandits gesticulated at him to get out of their way, but Joe started pointing at the pot of water they were boiling for coffee. When he wouldn't move one leapt to his feet and gave him a hard shove. Joe fell back on to the hard rock floor of the cave, cracking his head. He lay ominously still as the bandits laughed around him.

Michael's heart was in his mouth. The whole escape would be doomed if . . .

Joe rolled over. He was facing Michael now. His eyes

opened. They met his own. He was OK.

Joe suddenly jumped back to his feet and started yelling and waving his fists at the bandit who'd pushed him over. They all seemed to find this even funnier than him being knocked down. But then Joe swung his foot at the boiling pot, upending it and dousing the flames in one swift, fluid movement. Barely a fraction of a second later Michael whipped out the T-shirt he'd picked up and threw it over the other smaller fire, covering the flames and then crushing it down with his foot to extinguish them.

Pitch black!

As pandemonium erupted behind him, Michael charged towards the river.

Chapter Twenty

Katya was less than a metre from the water — so close that she could almost taste it — when the cave seemed to explode into light, blinding her and stopping her in her tracks. Beside her Dr Roper stumbled and would have fallen if Joe's mother hadn't caught her. Michael slid to a halt beside them. Joe was a dozen metres back. High-powered beams enveloped them from the other side of the river, and they knew their escape attempt was over.

'Going somewhere?'

It was a voice Katya recognized. She forced herself to look towards its source, shielding her eyes with one hand until she grew more accustomed to the brightness. The speaker was wearing a white suit, trainers and a baseball cap. His hair was cut shorter and dyed blonder, but there was no mistaking the leader of the gang who'd tried to intimidate the Artists when they'd first arrived on the island. Then his suit had been frayed and mud flecked; this one was in better shape, whiter, but the hems were still thick with dust.

The original bandits swarmed up behind Katya and Michael, Joe and the two women and grabbed them, shouting and screaming, but also casting fearful glances towards their boss and ten more of his henchmen across the river. He must have emerged from a different tunnel further upstream – but there was no obvious point for him to cross. He pointed at one of the men holding Michael and began to talk quickly. The man looked terrified.

'What's happening?' Katya whispered to Joe.

'Boss man Mr Jaya not happy with who he left in charge. Man he left in charge not happy with being left for so long. Man is stupid, Mr Jaya doesn't like being argued with, everyone knows that.'

Mr Jaya, thought Michael. It was good to have a name.

Mr Jaya barked a command to the other bandits, and they immediately grabbed the man he had been arguing with and dragged him to the river's edge. Mr Jaya produced a pistol and aimed it directly at the man, who immediately sank to his knees and began crying and wailing. He was begging for his life.

Mr Jaya hesitated. He lowered his pistol. The man uttered his thanks. But Mr Jaya wasn't finished. He issued another instruction, and immediately the man was picked up and hurled into the swollen river.

But he was not flushed away in the manner that they had imagined for themselves.

At the very instant he splashed into the river he gave out a blood-curdling scream and disappeared in a hiss of steam, instantly scalded to death by the boiling water.

Katya couldn't get the image out of her head. He had held them prisoner, and might well have killed them if so ordered by Mr Jaya, but nobody, *nobody* deserved to die like that. And but for the good timing of Mr Jaya's unexpected arrival, they would have suffered an identical fate. She was shaken, and frightened and horrified – she wanted to scream at Mr Jaya: 'You *monster!*'

But the words would not come. He had a thin smile on his lips. When he spoke, he almost sounded as if he was purring.

'I am thinking the great Dr Kincaid will pay much money so that his children do not end up like *that.*'

'We aren't his children,' said Michael. 'We just work for him.'

'In the west, children do not work.'

'In the west we do not kidnap children and threaten to kill them!' Katya shouted, suddenly finding her voice.

'No one is going to pay anything for us,' said Michael. 'That's not how SOS works!'

'You really think he will leave you to die?'

'If he has to!'

'Or do you think he will rescue you?'

Katya glared at him.

Mr Jaya's smile grew wider. 'If you were hoping for that, then you will be very disappointed. At this moment your father is two hundred miles away. He thinks he is trailing me to my headquarters, to where I keep my prisoners. Every step he takes, I know about it! He is a foolish man who thinks he knows everything!'

'He's not as dumb as you look,' said Michael.

Mr Jaya's brow furrowed. Before he could properly translate it Katya joined in.

'If you had any sense you wouldn't even be thinking about the money right now, you'd be thinking about protecting your investment, about getting us out of here before this mountain blows up.'

'*This* mountain? I think not. I grew up here, I know its ways.'

'This is a *volcano*,' snapped Katya. 'It *is* going to erupt, and very soon, and we will all be killed.'

Mr Jaya shook his head. 'I am not stupid! I know of SOS and their ways. I know that they cannot find us here. If we go outside – satellites, thermal imaging, electronic tags, all will combine to expose us. But not under here. Not in my mountain. Not in the halls of the mighty Taron! This is my spiritual home! Home of the Duk-Duk!'

'You are not Duk-Duk.'

Katya turned. Joe had moved up to join them.

'You are not Duk-Duk!' he spat. 'You are evil. Duk-Duk is for good, Duk-Duk is to help people, and keep ancient law. But you burn. You destroy. You murder.'

Michael thought it was extraordinarily brave. Of them all, Joe was the most vulnerable. There was no ransom to be paid for him, no SOS team searching for him. Mr Jaya had no reason to keep him alive, and every reason to kill him.

'Joe . . .' said Katya.

Joe kept his eyes on Mr Jaya. 'You are not Duk-Duk. My father was Duk-Duk. You killed my father.'

'Yes I did,' said Mr Jaya, his voice perfectly calm, 'just as I will now kill you.'

He began to move his gun up again – but then stopped, and his mouth opened in surprise.

Michael glanced to his right.

Joe was standing with his legs slightly apart, for perfect balance, and with his two hands raised and joined around the handle of the SOS Browning handgun, which he was now aiming directly at Mr Jaya's chest.

Michael looked even further back, to the bandits' fire, and could now see the bandit who had claimed their gun lying face down on the floor of the cave, ignored in the panic and melee of their attempted escape. Joe had done more than douse the fire. Instead of running straight for the river he had zeroed in on the gunman, felled him in the dark and liberated their weapon.

Mr Jaya quickly recovered his composure. He gave a slight shake of his head. 'You have one gun, I have ten on this side of the river, and fifteen over there. You are surrounded, you are outgunned.'

But neither Joe's gun nor his resolve wavered.

Mr Jaya's men had now realized what was going on and those who had guns were aiming at Joe, while the others had their machetes raised and ready to attack. But no one was going to make a move before Mr Jaya gave the nod – and that wasn't going to happen, because he knew if the shooting started, he would be the first to go down.

Joe kept his eyes fixed on the bandit leader. 'Michael, Katya,' he said, 'take Dr Roper and my mother, and go.'

'Joe . . .' Katya began. 'You have to come with us.'

'Go!'

'No, we can't . . .'

Michael touched Katya's arm. 'We're only safe as long as he has Jaya in his sights.'

Katya looked distraught. 'But—'

'Katya, we have to go. It's our only chance.'

Joe's mother suddenly seemed to realize what was going on. She began to rush towards her son, talking rapidly. But Joe moved one hand off the gun and held it palm out and snapped, 'No!'

She stopped immediately. He spoke rapidly in his own language, and tears sprang from her eyes. Katya moved to her side and guided her away. Michael took hold of Dr Roper. 'C'mon, ' he said, 'your brother is waiting.'

She nodded vaguely at that, and began to walk,

holding on to his arm for support.

As they moved away from bandits along the side of the river, Michael looked back at Joe, still standing directly opposite Mr Jaya, both hands back on the gun.

What could he say? Joe was sacrificing himself, buying them time to get out of the cave and away from the mountain. There was no combination of circumstances that Michael could imagine that would result in Joe getting out alive.

'Thanks, Joe,' Katya called back, knowing how inadequate it was.

'See you later,' said Michael.

They both felt *awful.*

But they kept walking.

Ten minutes later, a single gunshot echoed along the tunnel.

Then about thirty others.

Joe was dead.

And the chase was on.

Chapter Twenty-One

As soon as Michael heard the gunshots reverberate he realized the fatal flaw in their plan. The cave tunnel was like a giant amplifier feeding sound towards the entrance.

'Kill the light,' he snapped.

'I can't, we won't be able to—'

'Do it!'

Normally Katya would have made a point of *not* doing something Michael ordered. But not now, not under these circumstances. She flipped the light off and immediately they seemed to wink out of existence.

Dr Roper cried out. Joe's mother said something soothing.

Katya said, 'They're getting closer. What's . . . ?'

Michael reached out in the dark, feeling for her.

He caught her arm and pulled her closer.

'The guard at the entrance,' he hissed. 'He'll have heard the shots.'

'We can't just stop.'

'Nope. But let's not give him something to shoot at.'

They moved ahead. They had the river on one side as some kind of guide, but the utter darkness made it impossible to move at anything other than a snail's pace. Dr Roper was weak and could hardly walk, even with Joe's mother's support. They could hear the excited cries of their pursuers thanks again to the cave's acoustics, but not yet see the light from their torches, although this had more to do with the twisting nature of the cave than any lack of proximity.

Michael squeezed Katya's arm. 'There . . .' he whispered. 'Light . . .'

It was ahead of them, a beam moving up and down, sideways. The guard from the entrance had become curious about the sounds coming towards him, but was unable to communicate with his comrades due to the lack of a mobile phone signal.

They knew there was no way of just sneaking past him.

'We need to take him out,' said Katya.

'No choice.'

'We need bait.'

'We do.'

They whispered briefly, agreed their strategy, then moved Dr Roper and Joe's mother to the very edge of the boiling river and made them lie down flat. Katya moved further up the cave towards the oncoming light. Michael skirted the wall, feeling it with his hands, desperately searching for some kind of a gap, something he could step or climb into to take him out of the path of the approaching beam.

'Hurry,' Katya whispered.

'Doing my best . . .'

His hands slipped across the damp limestone, the damp *warm* limestone. He could actually feel it vibrating.

Dr Roper, descending deeper into the delirium of a malarial fever, began to cry, 'Where's my brother? Where's my . . . ?' before her voice was suddenly muffled.

Michael felt a gap in the cave wall. He reached blindly into it – empty space. It might only go back a few metres, or stretch for kilometres into the very heart of the mountain. But it was enough for him to slip into.

'*Now*,' he hissed.

He couldn't see Katya, but he knew what she was doing. She had dropped to her knees parallel to him, and then stretched out, face up so that it would catch the light. She lay, waiting and watching, as the beam drew closer and closer, sticking mostly to the ground but every few metres racing up the walls and across the ceiling then back down on to the path. Finally, it fell on her.

The bandit stopped. He shouted something. There was no response, no sound other than the bubbled hiss of the river. His beam ranged across the ground around her, then up and across the walls. Michael held his breath as the light crossed the gap and continued back to Katya.

The bandit moved right up, until he was standing over her. He shone his flashlight down on to her still face and closed eyes before poking her with his toe. She remained deathly still.

He did it again.

This time her foot flashed out and swept the legs from under him. The bandit hit the hard cave floor on his left hip and let out a yelp of pain. The flashlight dropped from his hand and rolled away, but stayed on, bathing the cave in enough light for him to see

Katya jump to her feet. He may have dropped the torch, but he'd held on to his gun. He pulled it up sharply, gripped expertly in two hands, and would have shot her dead if Michael hadn't kicked it from his grasp. As it clattered away they both landed on him, Katya punching him once, hard, in the groin. His head jerked up just in time to meet Michael's knee, rocking it right back again, cracking the back of his skull hard against the limestone and knocking him out.

It couldn't have gone better, but there was no time to savour the success of their ambush. Shouts and yells came from behind, and for the first time they saw the lights of their pursuers, and the giant shadows they threw on the walls of the cave.

Katya picked up the bandit's torch. Michael secured his gun. Joe's mother helped Dr Roper back to her feet and encouraged her forward. But there was no hurry left in her. Joe's Mother turned pleading eyes to Michael – she knew, and he knew, that Dr Roper was going to get them all killed.

Unless.

Katya was already moving, doing her best to shepherd the women along, when she realized that Michael wasn't following.

'Michael?'

He stood where he was, facing back down the cave. 'You go on,' he said.

'*What?* What are you talking about? Come *on*!'

'I can't! Katya – they'll catch us and kill us all. You know they will. I have the gun, I can pin them down, buy you some time to get out.'

'No! Shoot at them as we move!'

'No, Katya! They'll keep after us, and even if we make the entrance, they'll be able to pick us off on the climb down. The only way to stop them is to make a stand here. It's the only way.'

'Michael!'

'We came here to rescue Dr Roper – that's what we're doing.'

'Michael!'

'Just do it! I'll keep them here until I run out of bullets and then I'll run for it. I'll be fine.'

Their pursuers were getting louder, closer, their shadows jumbled together on the walls like one single entity with dozens of arms and legs scrambling towards them. She knew what he was saying made sense. They were SOS. They were on a mission. They put themselves in the way of danger to help other people, animals, environments. And they only had one gun. There was no point in both of them staying. But every cell in her body wanted to stand where he was, with him, and fight.

But she would go. She would desert him. She had no choice.

'See you in a few minutes,' said Michael.

'Not if I see you first.'

Dr Roper and Joe's mother had advanced just half a dozen metres. Michael and Katya both knew that he was going to have to buy more than a few minutes if they were going to have any chance at all of exiting the cave and climbing down beside the waterfall.

She nodded at him once before turning. She angled the flashlight to the ground to light their way, her heart thumping hard and a desperate sense of betrayal weighing her down.

Chapter Twenty-Two

Michael took the spare flashlight and rolled it along the floor of the cave. That way, when they started shooting, it would be at the light and not at him. He retook his position in the alcove, leant out and shot once back down the tunnel. There was an immediate panic, retreat and a dousing of his pursuers' flashlights. The only light now came from his torch. At least until about thirty bullets cracked into it, turning it into shrapnel which peppered the wall and plunged everything into darkness.

It was an impasse. He was without light, and they were too scared of getting shot to turn theirs on. What he would have given for the night scope, but it had been left behind by the campfire as the bandits scattered their possessions.

And then he had a chilling thought.

What if they had found the scope? Even now one of them might be moving through the pitch black towards him. He wouldn't know a thing about it until a gun was placed against his head.

No, *no* – they hadn't recognized the scope for what it was when they'd first discovered it, there was no reason for them to now suddenly understand what it was. They were as blind as he was.

He could conceivably sneak off now, catch up with Katya while the bandits presumed they were pinned down. A big part of him wanted to do just that. But *no*. It was so intensely black now that he couldn't see his hand in front of his face. If he tried to follow Katya the chances were that he would either crack his head off the cave wall or stumble over a rock and fall into the boiling waters. He had thought he was being exceedingly cunning by drawing the bandits' fire to his torch, but all he had done was destroy his one source of light. He had to stick to the plan. The longer he kept them at bay, the more time Katya would have to lead Dr Roper and Joe's mother to safety.

Joe. Poor Joe. If he had managed to shoot Mr Jaya, before going down in a hail of bullets, the bandits might now be not much more than a disorganized, angry rabble. They might not be after their escaped hostages at all, but merely trying to escape from the mountain by the quickest possible route. But he was quite certain they would take time out of their flight to kill him and Katya and Dr Roper and Joe's mother. They wouldn't want to leave any witnesses alive. Murder them, leave their bodies for the volcano to consume. If, on the other hand, by some miracle Mr Jaya was still alive, and his men had managed to kill Joe before he could shoot him, then the bandit leader was more than capable of inspiring enough fear in his men that they were prepared to ignore the erupting mountain and hurl themselves after the escaping hostages.

Michael ran his fingers over the gun. How many bullets did he have? How long had he been standing there now? Five minutes? Ten?

He listened.

The hiss and pop of the river.

The tom-tom thump of his own heart.

But what of the bandits?

Nothing.

No light, no noise.

What if they'd worked out how to cross the river, and were exiting the cave by whatever tunnel Mr Jaya had used to enter?

He did have one source of light – he held it in his hands. It would mean wasting another bullet, but he had to find out what was happening.

Michael raised the gun, and squeezed the trigger.

The weapon boomed and bucked in his hand. As the sound reverberated the tunnel was illuminated for just a fraction of a second, but it was enough to terrify him.

The floor of the cave was *alive*.

The bandits were crawling along on their bellies towards him and were not more than twenty metres away. One of them was way out in front and with the night scope raised. The only reason he hadn't spotted Michael yet was because he remained out of his line of sight in the alcove. But that would change in a matter of seconds.

He had to move *now*.

Michael fired twice into the tunnel before turning and running as fast as he possibly could. All around him bullets exploded, and the flash of the muzzles both lit his way and guided their aim. Something bit into his arm, and he spun and fell and rolled and it was only by pure luck that he brained himself on a rock rather than plunging into the boiling water.

Shot, I'm shot, I'm shot in the arm and they're

coming, they're coming, they see me, I'm dead, I'm dead, I'm dead . . .

His head was scrambled, they were still shooting and now they were up and running towards him. Michael tried to get to his feet, but the ground seemed to shift under him, and he thought it was his dying muscles giving way. He raised his gun and shot blindly. In the flash of the discharge he saw the bandit with the night scope suddenly stagger and fall, less than five metres from him. Wearing the scope had not only allowed him to see in the dark, but also given him a misplaced confidence. Instead of protecting himself and approaching cautiously he had charged at Michael, determined to claim the glory, and been accidentally shot down for his foolishness.

Michael fired four more times, causing his pursuers to throw themselves down again. He pinpointed the downed bandit and as soon as the light faded he crawled forward until he collided with his body, felt around it until he located the scope and then rolled away. He got to his knees and raised the scope. He could see! Twenty bandits were slowly rising, venturing forward. Michael forced himself up. He stumbled forward. He fell. He got up. The ground was *moving*. He ran, he ran and he *ran*.

There.

The mouth of the cave. He had prayed for broad daylight and a cool breeze, but there was just a dull grey and the same stifling heat. He staggered into the entrance. The waterfall was to his left, but he only knew that because he could hear it. His view of *everything* was obliterated by falling ash, great swirling sheets of it. For the moment, standing where he was, he was sheltered from it, but he had no choice but to begin the climb down. He stepped out, gasping as the hot, acrid air burned his throat, and was immediately swallowed up. He might have considered it a blessing that the ash was masking his descent from his pursuers, but it was choking and blinding him, making it difficult to pick out his steps. The night scope was useless now, the gun was empty. He threw them away. From somewhere above he heard cries and yells and knew that the bandits had reached the exit.

Keep going.

Keep going.

Keep . . . going.

Michael reached the bottom of the waterfall. He sank to his knees, torn by a coughing fit. His arm was dead. He couldn't breathe. The ash was so thick he couldn't tell which way to go.

As he gasped on the thick carpet of ash, he thought of Katya. She was out there somewhere with Dr Roper and Joe's mother. He prayed that they hadn't been caught in *this*. There was no way that Dr Roper could have handled it, and Katya wouldn't have left her; so maybe they were all dead, lying suffocated under it.

Just like me.

No!

If I stay here I'm dead.

Get up.

Get up!

You're SOS!

If Katya was here, she'd kick your butt.

They all would!

Mr Crown would haul you up by the throat and make you run!

So BLOODY RUN!

Michael dragged himself up.

He forced one foot forward, and then the other.

He made perhaps another twenty metres before a flaming rock exploded to his left and knocked him sideways. He rolled and let out a yelp of pain as his wounded arm smacked against the ground. He sat up. He tried to breathe. He sucked in more ash than air.

He was choking. He lay on his back. He felt a warm blast of air and for a moment the ash was sucked away and his field of vision cleared.

And he wished it hadn't.

For what he was seeing was surely a vision of hell.

He was halfway down the incline they had climbed to reach the cave. All of the vegetation for as far as he could see was burning. Flaming rocks were landing and exploding like mortar shells *everywhere*. The river was no longer flowing swiftly, but was choked with mud and boiling up over its banks and beginning to flood. The heat of Mount Taron was so intense that it was creating its own weather system, with lightning flashing out and hot rain pelting down. The wind shifted again, and for the first time he noticed a rough track, hidden on their night-time approach and winding away in the opposite direction. About a kilometre away he had the briefest glimpse of half a dozen parked cars, all of them burning furiously.

And then the curtain of ash closed again, thicker than ever, and whatever vague ghostly light there had been was extinguished.

He couldn't move. He was exhausted, he was shot, he couldn't breathe.

He was dying.

He was *dying*.

In moments he would blink out of existence.

His body would never be found.

The ash would bury him, and harden, and molten rock would flow over him. He would become part of Mount Taron. Part of the earth and dust and atoms that made up everything.

NO!!

He forced himself to sit up again.

'I will not die,' he said, his voice rough and raspy. 'I will . . . not . . . die . . .' He was racked by a coughing fit. The ash was in his mouth, his throat, his nose, his lungs. 'I will not . . . die! I will not die . . . I will not die . . . I will not die . . . I WILL NOT BLOODY BLOODY DIE!' he screamed, one last useless act of defiance before he was consumed.

Beside him a quiet, slightly muffled voice said, 'OK. But no need to yell.'

Chapter Twenty-Three

'So, apparently, you WILL NOT DIE.'

The voice was Katya's, but not the one he had heard on the mountain. *That* had belonged to Bailey, resplendent in a fireproof suit, and Bonsoir beside him, helping to pick him up and carry him through the ash and molten boulders towards what had to be the most bizarre vehicle he had ever seen. Later he would learn that it was an ex-army armoured personnel carrier retro-fitted with huge, solid flame-resistant tyres that allowed it to almost bounce its way through difficult terrain. It had been airlifted in by SOS for situations *exactly* like this.

As soon as he was bundled into the back a bottle of water was poured over his head to clear the ash, and then he was handed another to wash out his mouth. As he gargled and spat Katya said, 'Don't mind us, just spit wherever you feel like.'

Her sarcasm was familiar, and strangely, very welcome. He had thought she was dead. He had thought *he* was dead. His throat was ragged and sore and he could barely swallow. He blinked at her through eyelashes still clogged with volcanic dust. She was also smeared with a mixture of water and ash, but otherwise looked uninjured. There too was Dr Roper, curled up in a ball, with an oxygen mask clamped to her face. And Joe's mother was slumped beside her.

'*How* . . . ?' Michael croaked.

'Tracking device in our trainers,' said Katya. 'As soon as we exited the mountain they were on to us.'

Michael peered forward. Bailey was driving, with his face mask pushed up and suit hood thrown back. But he was driving blind, his vision obscured by the ash. His windscreen wipers were working hard, but might as well not have been working at all for all the difference they were making.

'How . . . do you know where we're going . . . what if . . . what if . . . ?' Michael's voice gave out.

Bailey smiled back. 'Instinct,' he said. And then after a moment, 'And sat nav. Though not the kind you're going to buy in your friendly neighbourhood computer store. This is military. This is good. This is fun.'

Michael's head lolled back. He felt weak, dizzy, disorientated, though part of that was the bouncing of the vehicle and the sudden shouts of surprise that came as they crashed into something unexpected. His eyes moved towards Kayta.

'The volcano . . .' he whispered.

'Is erupting, yes,' said Katya. 'Bonsoir, how long until we reach St Mark's?'

The master planner glanced back. 'We're just trying to outrun this ash for now. There's a new weather system coming in, the wind will likely change direction, make our progress a bit easier. We've been lucky so far. A lot of molten rocks and ash are being flung out, there are several lava flows, the smoke funnel is half a mile into the sky, but there's been no massive eruption. It could all calm down pretty quickly – or it could just suddenly detonate. We're not out of the woods yet.'

'Joe?' Michael asked.

Katya said something, but he didn't quite hear it. Everything was starting to sound muffled.

'Joe?' he asked again.

'I told you,' Katya hissed in his ear, 'don't mention him, his mother . . .'

Michael's eyes flitted to her. She was staring straight

ahead, dead-eyed.

'The only reason we're here,' said Katya, 'is because of what Joe did. He sacrificed himself.'

'Hero,' said Michael.

'Hero,' said Katya.

Michael's head slumped down on his chest. He forced it back up again. He saw a superior kind of grin on her face.

'What?'

'You're not so tough.'

'OK.' He was too tired to argue.

'You look like death warmed up.'

'I'm just . . .'

There was something at the back of his mind that he knew he was supposed to have mentioned to his rescuers, but he couldn't quite pinpoint it.

'You're just useless.'

'Yeah . . . suppose . . .'

'And you're agreeing with me! One little cloud of ash and you fall to pieces. I seriously doubt you have a future with SOS.'

'I . . .'

Michael remembered running. He remembered choking. He remembered thinking he was done for. Now here he was, safe, a survivor. He had escaped from a volcano. Dr Roper was safe, and so their mission was accomplished.

Everything was OK.

Fine.

Except, something was still nagging at him.

Oh yes. It came to him.

He said, 'We're going to St Mark's?'

Bonsoir nodded back. 'Dr Kincaid, Mr Crown and Dr Faustus are meeting us there. Why?'

'No . . . reason. Hospital. Just – I think I might have been shot.'

Michael turned stiffly in his seat to show them his arm. It was caked in a thick layer of ash which had stuck to it in a way it hadn't with the others; it was the blood, oozing as thick and sticky and poisoned as the river flooding the rainforest around Mount Taron.

Things got even hazier. He was looking at Katya, but she was swimming in and out of focus. She was examining his arm, but he was concentrating on her face, and the way there seemed to be tears coursing down her cheeks, but he was pretty sure he was imagining that.

Chapter Twenty-Four

They watched in awe and fear as the south face of Mount Taron was swept away in a sudden and explosive torrent of lava which began to roll cross-country, consuming everything in its path. As it progressed it began to narrow into a single winding channel which nevertheless seemed intent on flowing right over the beleaguered little community stranded at St Mark's Mission Station.

The eruption, with all the power of an atomic bomb, had been shocking enough, and the speed and fury of it had mesmerized them all; but there was something even more frightening about what was now moving towards them: in lava terms it was extremely fast, but actually watching the flow it appeared relatively slow – perhaps a kilometre or so every hour. But it was *relentlessly* moving in their direction, and there was nothing they could do to stop it and no possibility of escape. The swollen river had burst its banks, destroying the few bridges that crossed it and flooding the land all around. The water was too thick with debris and the current too strong for even the largest and most powerful boats. Although they now had a fair view of the mountain, the air was still too thick with ash to allow rescue by air. St Mark's was on a slightly elevated piece of land, and it had saved them. But it also held them captive. They were prisoners with a death sentence.

They watched it all from the dubious shelter of the hospital. A local volunteer was on the roof, putting out fires. Dr Kincaid sat by his sister's bed, holding her hand, as she valiantly fought against her insidious malarial infection. Dr Faustus and Dr Leota between them were looking after the patients who could not be evacuated in the hours leading up to the eruption, and now it was too late.

Michael was in bed too, his arm bandaged and his head woozy from the anaesthetic and painkillers. The bullet was sitting on the small locker beside him, a souvenir of his time under the mountain. Katya had spent a lot of time in a chair by his side, but now that he was awake she appeared to have forgotten that he was recovering from surgery and was instead blitzing him with random information about the differing speeds of lava flow and why this particular type was moving so quickly.

Eventually he said, 'Nobody likes a know-all. Fortunately we're all going to die soon and all your facts and figures will perish with us.'

Katya made a face before getting up and squeezing herself into a position by the window. The hospital was packed, not just with patients and staff, but also dozens of people seeking refuge from the floods. It was a grey world and the only colour came from the red-tinged lava, glowing and twisting like an enormous snake escaping from the chambers of hell.

For a moment her view was blocked as an enormous figure passed in front of the window. Then as it stepped away she saw who it was: Mr Crown. He was facing the hospital rather than the lava; he had his shirt off and a shovel in his hands.

'Right!' he bellowed. 'I want every single one of you who can walk, who can lift so much as a spoon, out here right now. This lava is coming. We're not just going to lie down and let it take us. We're going to build a defensive wall, we're going to dig channels and trenches, we're going to fight until there's not an ounce of strength in us. So get out here . . . NOW!'

Katya glanced up. Bailey was beside her. 'There's no point,' she said. 'It'll be like building a sandcastle on the beach. The tide always comes in and washes it away.'

Bailey smiled. 'Maybe. But isn't it fun building them?' He winked. 'Come on. What else are you going to do, hang around making big eyes at him?' He nodded down at Michael.

'As if,' said Katya.

As she began to follow Bailey and the others outside Michael threw his cover off and swung his legs down.

'You stay where you are.' It was Dr Faustus.

Michael just looked at him.

Dr Leota came up beside Dr Faustus. He looked at Michael. 'Would you like a second opinion, son?'

Michael nodded. Dr Leota looked at Dr Faustus. 'I concur, Doctor. He's too weak.'

That was like a red rag to a bull. Michael stood up. Then he sat down again. Then he gathered his strength and regained his feet.

'I'm not lying in bed while everyone else helps.'

Dr Faustus said, 'Fair enough.'

'I concur again,' said Dr Leota.

Michael thought they seemed unduly upbeat,

bearing in mind what was approaching. He supposed that everyone had their own way of dealing with impending death. Mr Crown was defiant, Bailey was resigned but funny with it, the two medical doctors were flippant and Dr Kincaid . . . well, he remained by his sister's bed, staring into space.

Michael stopped in front of him. He said, 'I'm going out to dig.'

Dr Kincaid nodded vaguely. He looked somehow older, and beaten down. His eyes moved sluggishly towards Michael, and took a few moments to focus in properly. 'What was that?' he asked.

'I'm going outside to dig, Dr Kincaid. Are you joining us?'

His eyes flitted to his sister. 'You saved her,' he said. 'I went in completely the wrong direction.'

'We were lucky,' said Michael.

'Luck,' said Dr Kincaid. 'All the money in the world can't buy you luck. You seem to have it, son. But you're quite right. Not much point in saving my sister one minute and losing her to this damn lava the next.' He smiled and stood up. His eyes were suddenly clear again, the old sparkle was back. 'C'mon then! Let's get digging.'

* * *

Mr Crown provided the inspiration and the example, Bonsoir planned where and how high to build the barrier, and everyone else joined in the digging and building as best they could. There was only half a dozen spades between maybe thirty volunteers, so most had to use pieces of wood or kitchen utensils. The ground was soft and sandy for the most part, which made it easy to dig *in* to, but tree roots stretching across from the rainforest and dead roots dating back to when the land had been cleared to build the mission station made it difficult to loosen chunks of soil big enough to use in the construction of the wall. But they kept at it, and kept at it, and every time they paused for breath or to take a quick fearful glance at the advancing lava Mr Crown barked at them to get back to work. Though he tried his best Michael couldn't make much headway with his one good arm, and so Dr Faustus, himself using a grisly-looking surgical instrument to dig with, pulled him off the line and reassigned him to keep everyone supplied with water. The well St Mark's used was already polluted, so he was reduced to handing out cupfuls from a barrel filled with water recovered from different parts of the hospital and the few homes dotted about the settlement. It tasted vaguely of wood and ash – but was still more than welcome.

He made the trip to the barrel about twenty times, and was just turning away when he became aware of movement from the far side of their little island, behind the mission, where by right there should have been nothing. There was a sea of flotsam and jetsam out there preventing their escape: which should theoretically also have prevented anyone approaching, but there were, unmistakably, figures now moving quickly towards him. Michael shook his head, half believing that he was hallucinating because of the drugs he'd been given.

They drew closer, and closer, and when they were right up beside him he had another shock, because not only were they completely caked in mud, they were also wearing hideous masks, garishly painted with devil eyes. Michael should have shouted, raised the alarm that the bandits were back and were now attacking them, but he found himself utterly speechless. They breezed past him, moving swiftly towards the slowly rising wall and the line of workers before it. They stopped and stood in a line, saying nothing, until the locals, the walking wounded and the refugee villagers began to notice them, and as word spread they immediately stopped working and dropped to their knees and bowed down.

Dr Kincaid turned to face them, and looked suitably

shocked before raising a hand in greeting. Mr Crown moved beside him. His greeting was raising and pointing an automatic rifle.

There was a long moment when nothing was said. Michael was surprised to find Katya beside him. 'You recognize the masks? Duk-Duk.'

'What do you want?' said Mr Crown, his voice cool, fearless.

The Duk-Duk slightly to the front of the others pushed his mask up and off his face.

'We came to help,' he said.

It was Joe.

Katya enveloped him in a hug, but Joe hardly responded. There was something different about him. She felt it immediately and let him go. Taking a step back she said, 'Joe? We thought you were dead.'

'I am Duk-Duk now.'

Dr Kincaid moved closer. 'Katya – who is this? Why are all these people bowing down to them?'

'They are Duk-Duk,' said Katya. 'It's a secret society, it protects the people. This is Joe – bandits killed his father, burned his village. But he led us into the mountain, he saved Dr Roper.'

Dr Kincaid nodded at Joe. 'I thank you, all of

you, on behalf of my sister. But how . . . how did you get here?' He waved around him. The mission station was an island surrounded by water, deep mud and approaching lava.

'We were guided by the spirits,' said Joe. Michael waited for him to smile. He did not. 'We move from dry spot, to dry spot. We walk lightly. We wait. On the way we lose five men. But we are here. Here to build wall.'

'Well, that's exactly what we need,' said Mr Crown. He had no time for niceties. 'Grab what you can and get diggin'.' He turned away. 'C'mon!' he shouted to the others. 'Get off your knees and keep digging! This is our one chance, our only chance! Dig! Dig! Dig!'

Everyone got back to work. Even the rotund Father Damian left off praying in his church and got busy – using one end of a silver cross to scoop out the dirt.

'Not exactly what it was intended for,' he gasped, 'but I think the Lord would approve.'

Joe and the other Duk-Duks took their place in the line, right beside Katya. They worked silently and efficiently. Joe seemed older, more serious, as if he had turned from a boy into a man in the space of a few hours. He was so focused on what he was doing that Katya wasn't even comfortable with asking how he had escaped from the mountain. She glanced down at his burned ankles. Instead of being poisoned and swollen, they looked as if they were well on the way to recovery. She was pretty sure it wasn't her own poor attempt at treating them that had healed them so well – but she also knew there were lotions and potions in remote areas like this that were more powerful than conventional western medicine.

Michael had no such qualms about getting the truth out of Joe. When he next approached with water he said bluntly, 'How did you escape? We heard the shooting. We presumed you were dead.'

Joe, working with the edge of a large, flat stone, didn't pause for one moment, nor did he look up. But he spoke calmly and efficiently. 'I was wrong. I thought the people in my village were weak. When my father was murdered by the bandits, and I ran, I thought they gave in to them. But they did not. They pretended too, until they could find out where I was. Duk-Duk from the mountain told Duk-Duk from the village. But there are many caves. So they watched, and when Mr Jaya arrived, they followed him in, and saw the camp, and made a plan. And there was shooting and Mr Jaya fell in the river and died, and his men ran, most of them the way that you escaped, some into other tunnels. Duk-Duk brought wood with them to ford the river, and I left by different tunnel. We survive. We come here. I am chief of village now, leader of Duk-Duk. But that does not matter if we all die. We dig. We dig. We dig.'

They dug.

Before he turned to fetch more water Michael looked out over the slowly rising barrier at the river of lava moving relentlessly towards them, and he was gripped with a cataclysmic fear that it was all in vain, that nothing could stop it, that they were going to be overwhelmed.

But then he looked along the line, and a wave of defiant optimism swept through him. SOS was working side by side with the local refugees, with the hospital patients, with the man of God, Father Damian, with the Duk-Duk and whatever spirits they believed in, everyone working together with a common purpose – survival.

A metre down from him one of the hospital patients collapsed suddenly, exhausted. As Dr Faustus bent to examine him, Michael gently prised the spade from his fingers. He was done with carrying water. He rejoined the line, right beside Katya and Joe, ignoring the blood that was seeping through his bandaged arm, and he started digging.

Chapter Twenty-Five

Someone was shaking his arm – his good arm – gently. Michael tried to open his eyes, but dirt and ash had glued them shut. As he worked at them Katya said, 'Michael – come on.'

Gradually the world hove back into view. Katya was on her haunches beside him, her face smeared as badly as his.

'What . . . *what?*'

'Come see.'

He was stretched out under the protective wall, which now stood at least a metre above him. It was no longer dark, but neither was it exactly bright. He guessed it was dawn, because there was a hint of brightness in the sky, but the sunlight was too weak to fully break through the mist and smoke which hung over everything. Michael looked along the base of the barrier. He wasn't the only one to have collapsed from exhaustion. It looked like the aftermath of a battle, or the dying minutes of a siege. But the fact that it looked like *anything* at least meant that they were all still alive, that they had not yet been overwhelmed.

'Come *on*, lazy bones.'

Katya put out her hand and helped to drag him up. Michael began to stretch, but before he could fully extend himself she jerked him forward. There were footholes already dug into the wall. She climbed up before turning to help him. Michael looked at his bandage: thick with mud and blood. His arm wasn't particularly sore, just stiff. He held out his good hand, and she hauled him up. The top of the wall had been roughly flattened out and was wide enough along about half of its length to allow people to stand on it: and they were several already there. Dr Kincaid had a supportive arm around his sister, who had clearly passed the worst of her fever. Bailey was there, and Mr Crown, and Dr Faustus. Bonsoir was just clambering up, further along.

Michael stared out. It was as if someone had taken a photograph, freezing everything in different hues of grey. It was still a vision of destruction, but the waters had subsided, leaving behind a sea of steaming, stagnant mud. But the greatest threat, the river of molten lava, had, inexplicably, changed its course less than three hundred metres from St Mark's; it had crept past their little island for perhaps another half a kilometre before coming to a halt. The strength of its brutal tide had finally waned and now it lay motionless, glowing still but like the dying embers of a fire, hardly threatening at all.

'It just . . . stopped?' Michael asked.

'We were working so hard, we didn't even notice.'

The one small bell of St Mark's began to ring out, finally rousing everyone who hadn't already woken from their slumbers. They all peered up at the fire-damaged bell tower and saw Father Damian grinning out, punching the air and shouting, 'It's a miracle! It's a miracle!' before disappearing back to his ringing.

'Not a miracle,' said Bonsoir. 'Simply the laws of physics. It ran out of steam. It was going to happen sooner or later.'

'I'm just happy it happened sooner rather than later,' said Bailey.

'Close call,' said Dr Kincaid.

Only Mr Crown didn't look particularly happy. 'We would have beaten it,' he said, defiance etched on his smoke-blotched face.

Michael saw that Katya had a puzzled look on her face as she looked around her.

'What is it?'

'Joe. Where's Joe? And the rest of the Duk-Duk?'

'They left.' It was Dr Kincaid.

'Left?' said Katya. 'Just . . . left?'

'They helped us, and they left when it was safe for them to go.'

'But I didn't see them go.'

'You were sleeping.'

'I wasn't sleeping . . . I didn't . . . was I sleeping?'

'We were all sleeping at some point,' said Bailey, 'apart from *him*.' He nodded at Mr Crown. 'If I knew where he bought his batteries, I'd buy some for myself.'

'But Joe didn't say goodbye.'

'Yes, he did,' said Dr Kincaid.

Katya bit on her lip. She shook her head. 'He should have woken me.'

'He tried,' said Dr Kincaid.

'Dozer,' said Michael.

They heard the chopper a long time before they saw it. It grew louder and louder, finally dipping down out of the blanket of smoke that continued to hang over the rainforest in every direction as far as the eye could see.

The only one of the Artists who didn't look very pleased to see the SOS helicopter was Bailey.

'Who *the hell* is flying my bird?' he snapped. 'What if he breaks it?'

'Like you haven't ever done that,' said Bonsoir, shouting against the din.

'It's mine to break,' said Bailey.

'Actually,' said Dr Kincaid, 'it's *mine*.'

'Well, it's more mine than *his*!' Bailey shouted, nodding at the other pilot.

The helicopter settled in the ash-covered courtyard in front of the hospital. Patients' faces stared out of the windows, and all along the defensive wall the locals were clapping and cheering. An SOS team jumped out and immediately began unloading supplies of fresh water and food. Even though the rotor blades were slowing, the sound did not diminish: within a minute another SOS helicopter dropped down out of the sky, and then a third appeared.

Dr Kincaid pointed at it. 'Our ride's here, folks. Let's get moving.'

Michael looked at the devastation all around and at

the thirsty, hungry, exhausted locals who had helped build the defensive wall. He knew that most of them had fled from villages in the rainforest, that they had lost their homes, and members of their families, and perhaps their means of earning a living; that fresh food and water would be scarce, and with the roads and bridges destroyed by lava or the floods they were pretty much stranded here at St Mark's for the foreseeable future. He not only felt terribly sorry for them, but also dreadfully guilty.

He looked at Katya. 'We're just going to . . . leave?'

'Yes, Michael, it's time to go.'

'But these people . . . the hospital . . . what are they going to do?'

'Michael, we came for Dr Roper, that was our mission, and we've completed it. SOS support teams will take over for the next forty-eight hours, and then they'll make way for other relief agencies. You know that's how it works. We're the Artists, we go where we're needed.'

Michael took a deep breath. He knew what she was saying was right, that this was how SOS operated, but it still felt like they were taking the easy way out. He was conflicted: his arm was aching again, he was filthy and hungry and thirsty; he needed a complete rest. At least he had that option. Life for the people he was leaving behind would not be easy, but then it had never been easy. The rainforest was being devastated by loggers before he arrived, and then Mother Nature had stepped in and devastated it for herself. Soon the rainforest would start to grow again, the land would recover, and the people who lived there, the animals and birds and insects who relied upon it, would begin their battle for survival all over again. The bandits would return, and the Duk-Duk would fight them. Maybe Dr Roper would return as well.

Bailey had already taken possession of the controls of the helicopter.

'All aboard!' he shouted. 'Have your tickets ready for inspection!'

Dr Roper was helped onboard by her brother, while Mr Crown and the other Artists quickly loaded what remained of the supplies and equipment they had brought into the rainforest. As they worked, Dr Leota, Father Damian and many of the patients came up and said heartfelt goodbyes.

Bonsoir heaved Michael up into the body of the chopper, where he slumped down into a seat and with some difficulty strapped himself in. He closed his eyes and dozed quietly for just a few minutes until

Katya fell in beside him. She smiled. He wasn't used to her smiling at him.

'What's up with you?'

'Nothing,' she said. But there was definitely something. He shook his head. He wasn't being sucked into her trap. If she knew something, she could hold on to it for now. He was too tired to think or to play games.

The helicopter lifted off in a swirl of ash and debris and rose rapidly into the grey sky. As it skirted the collapsed and smoking Mount Taron Michael peered down at the destruction it had wrought on a broad swathe of the land surrounding it. It made the fact of their survival all the more remarkable.

It was a miracle.

Or luck.

He rested his head back and blew air out of his cheeks. He was looking forward to getting on to the SOS jet and a nice long sleep.

'It'll be good to get home,' he said quietly.

'Home?' said Katya. 'Don't you listen, empty-head? We're heading for Africa!'

'What? Africa? But, but, but, but . . . *why*?'

Katya grinned slyly, sat back and closed her eyes.

'Wait and see,' she said.